> OUR
> GORGEOUS
> JENBY FAIREY
>
> YOUR GAILE & I,
> OUR HOME N
> LOOKS the S
>
> ANDY & GAILE
> MARCH 18 2021.
> OXOXOOO
>
> JUST
> IT

In life there is one decision all of us need to make, that is paramount to where, and who you will one day become.

You simply have to select the right person in life, to support you 100% of the time.

That is a decision I made right, the first time, my dear wife of 49 years.

Thank you Gaile.

SPORT
IS the backbone to business

ANDREW BUYS

Copyright © 2019 Andrew Buys
All rights reserved
First Edition

PAGE PUBLISHING, INC.
New York, NY

First originally published by Page Publishing, Inc. 2019

ISBN 978-1-64462-957-4 (Paperback)
ISBN 978-1-64462-958-1 (Digital)

Printed in the United States of America

First, I have always been super-duper into sports and I wish to reflect how being sports minded has set me up with integrity (from my parents – and grand-parents- honor- reliability, politeness, and always being on time) this attention to detail and team sports sets up a good backbone for business. My being raised in a confined environment in Natal Command on the Snell Parade in the 1950 and 1963 environment, meant this small military community also molded my mind and how I was limited to make my way through life. Yes, I am also a military brat. My dad was a sergeant Major in the South African Army until he retired in 1972. I mention this for your understanding. It also meant I did not get to meet many girls, so I had no idea how to treat girls, so in that field I matured with girls much later than my school buddies. It also meant that my dad was not a businessman, so he could not share business ticktacks with me, I had to learn on the job and that takes many years longer; than with a businessman to show me, or to groom me.

So that this book would not be too complicated, I have divided this in two very different sections.

1). Section A is the sports side of my life from inception to the end of sport in my life
2). Section B is the business section from my first day at work in 1962 to the present day.

The reason for writing this book is to show sportsmen, or sports ladies, that once you are finished with sports, you have the tools imbedded in you to run your own business, even with little education. Your parents and; your environment, normally mold you for life, depending how you deal with these influences as you get older. Your "can do attitude" is far more important than your I.Q. On another aspect, I am a small built-man of 5 foot, 5 inches, and was always 132 lbs. My size just never came into any aspect of any sport I played. The soccer players I played with and against; were always far larger than me. The rugby players I played with were 280 pounds and I was 132, never once did size enter my mind. I made sure I was always faster, quicker off the mark, and super nimble, so I never ever sat on a bench. I was always far too valuable, not to be in the team 100 percent of the time. I was like a little puppy playing, tongue on the ground, tail wagging and very happy to be there. No wonder school suffered. **To view extra pictures related to this book enter www.arcbsports.com to your internet browser, then click to open.**

SECTION A

CHAPTER ONE

"The Red Rose Petal."

Our daughter Susan was twenty-nine years old, she had been married for two months when she found out she had cancer. The doctor told me this cancer was one; that no human had lived through. The name of this cancer is soft tissue sarcoma cancer. The doctor told me she had six months to live. Soft tissue sarcoma eats away at the tissue under your skin, then pops out of the skin. In Susan's case, the top left shoulder next to her collar-bone, the lump burst through the skin. Susan was determined to be the first person to live through this cancer, so she changed her eating habits to a raw-food diet, which means she only ate green food. This change of diet gave her and us two years together, but the cancer ball outside her skin had to be dressed twice each day and smelled bad. It was a large wet gooey mess, the size of a rugby ball, which is far larger than an American football, and part of this large bump tucked under her left arm. Even when it was small the doctors did not want to cut it out. Susan passed in December 2004, and she was cremated. Gaile, my wife of forty-eight years, held her ashes until one week-end in 2010. Debbie, my married daughter and her husband Richard, with their first son, Alexander, Gaile, and I took a trip to Peace River, Florida. Susan had asked her ashes to be spread there.

Peace River needs an over-night car trip to get there which we did. Reaching the canoe shop it was a typical canoe shop under eighty-year-old trees for shade, with canoes piled everywhere, kind of ram-shackled. One gentleman said your canoe is parked at the pier in the water ready for your day trip. The Five of us walked along the pier and carefully stepped into this canoe, handing Alexander from Mom to Granny in the canoe. Careful Gaile, with your first grand-child you may tip over and fall into the water. Andrew if this canoe tip's over then I will walk on water to keep Alexander safe. Okey-Doke. Richard (Debbie's wonderful husband) took the front with a paddle and did the right-hand side paddling, I was at the back doing all the left-hand side paddling. The River was slow, and we had elected to paddle up-river against a soft, slow meandering run of water. Each turn was gorgeous, and we were looking for a sandy beach where we could drag the canoe out the water and still have a nice beachy spot to say a few words. Riverbend after riverbend just showed us dense trees on the banks right up to the water-line on both sides. We had gone almost a mile when a wonderful spot appeared, it had the very beach we were looking for, so we drug the canoe well out of the water and the girls stood around doing what girls do when saying goodbye to their sister and daughter. I had bought 15 red and 15 white roses and once the ashes were emptied into the clear water, I plucked all the red petals off all the roses and did the same with all the white roses. Richard and I spread the rose petals onto the surface of the water where Gaile just put the ashes. There were lots of rose petals and no wind, so the rose petals kind of sat there, then the few petals on the end did a very slow circle and that circle got larger and larger, with more and more rose petals being picked up by a slow current of water making their way down from where we had come. When we left by canoe, there were lots of red and white rose petals over the spot and many more had been taken down river. I noticed a few stuck on the bank and suggested we play a game to see who could see the last rose petal. There's one, there's one then one stuck against a log on the bank, around a corner they were getting sparse, then the next corner even sparser, Debbie saw a white one a few minutes later Gaile saw another then around another corner and no rose petals, oh there is one and round the next corner. Then it was obvious that we were not going to find any more rose petals. We enjoyed the canoe and the quiet river around a few more bends. We rounded the final corner to see our dock 50 yards down from us and were prepared to carefully navigate across the river to meet our home dock. There were three columns into the water holding up the dock, on the middle column floating against this middle round column was **one red rose petal**. WOW now how about that. Now that was some unusual ending to our goodbye to our daughter Susan.

1946/7:

The beginning as far back as I remember. I was born in 1943.

The first memories. Playing with a scorpion in our outside garage, age 2 or 3 years old, yes it stung me as I picked it up, with my fingers and it hurt like hell. The next memory I have was falling off the roof of our garage where the scorpion stung me. Both my feet were broken, since then both my feet have always been wider than normal. Age 3 years old, we stayed in the house on ROSE STREET PRETORIA South Africa, corner plot. The house faced Rose Street and the garage faced the other road. ROUND 1947, we moved to Robert's Heights where seventeen years later I would be in the army doing mandatory military training and in 1963 Roberts heights was called Diensfack-skool (Services School).

The only memories I have of Robert's heights was the new Vampire jet air planes of the day. The new Vampires were unique because they had two thoraxes that ran from both front wings down to the tail of the plane, so the Vampires were easy to see up in the sky. One day my mom Nancy had dressed us 3 children for some event she had to take us on, and I got hold of black shoe polish and put it on to Dawn, Diane's and my arms and legs and remember my mom burst out crying. I have no idea if we went or stayed at home. My dad William Spencer Buys was doing poorly health wise and was given a few days to live so his doctor said he should go down to Durban as the weather was always warm on the coast. My dad had been wounded 5 times during world war 2 and never regained normal health. There was no post for my Dad at Natal Command, and they did not expect him to live to long, so we lived at the Carnarvon Hotel, which was very close to Windsor Park school. The three of use Dawn, Diane and myself all went to school at Windsor Park round November 1950. I could walk home after school. After the Carnarvon Hotel we were given a home with 102 steps in <u>Red Hill March</u> 1951 and my parents took us to school each day and we got home by bus each day, then walked up 102 steps every day. I do remember those **102** steps each day, as the bus-stop was at our front gate. We all went to school with satchel on our backs, which contained sandwiches for lunch at school. Off to school to learn the golden rule. Our mom would wake us with the following statement almost daily. Wakie, wakie rise and shine, it's school today and the weather is fine.

I realized far later in life that Windsor Park was shaping me for life. Being a tad smaller than all the children in my class I learned very early that boys are timid up to the age of 9-15, so in my first few days at Windsor Park I would be aggressive, and the bigger guys would cave. This stopped in High school, but the aggressive backbone was set in my life. I remember Windsor Park school, Grade one, Grade two, Standard 1 Standard 2 Standard 3 Standard 4 standard 5 and Standard 6 to be games, sports, marbles, stingers, soccer and Cricket to be a major part of my everyday life. School work was not important. Sports was what interested me. The first party I went to was at Raymond Broads home and I remember two girls running after Anthony van den Heuvel and myself. Later that evening Anthony said to me, "Andy we are going to the banana trees at the foot of the garden to smoke pot." I do not do that Ant, Andrew you got to come with us, so I said OK I'll come with you and Raymond, but I cannot smoke pot." I had heard my Dad proudly say, my son does not do that. I would not let my Dad down. We went to the Banana trees and they smoked, but not I. I have never done that in my life. I dropped out of School in Standard 8 (to Americans, this is grad 10). During these years my entire family would go to my Grand Parents farm in Kirkwood 50 miles from Port Elizabeth. My Uncle Douglas was killed in World War 2 and I inherited his pellet gun (an air rifle.) My grand Pa would sit on his porch, with the pellet gun (air gun) and at twilight time shoot the mice that ran along the 4 feet high hedge separating his land from the front sandy road. He encouraged me to shoot the birds that ate his figs on the farm. Grand Pa can I shoot a wild duck and kill it with the pellet gun, No, boy that wild duck is too tough for this old pellet gun (air gun). OK so daily I would enter the bush with pellets in my pocket and my pellet gun I did shoot many birds. I must have been 12-or 15 years old and my little sister Diane walked with me down to the river one late afternoon. I happened to be standing in the 6-inch-deep water and in a pool just ahead of Diane and myself two wild ducks flew in and settled on the calm glassy water. I had to bend down to get a view at the duck nearest to me, because some thick tree, full of leaves hampered my view of the duck. As I got a clear view of the duck closet to me, the duck bent down, and its tail stood up like a triangle above the water, I pulled the trigger. The duck did not move it just flopped forward and slowly floated down to me. I picked up the duck by the neck and ran with Diane behind me, Grand Pa I got a duck with my pellet gun, super proudly. We had duck for dinner that night. I had hit the poor duck on the lip of his butt and that must have paralyzed the bird.

I never shot birds once we stopped going to the farm. I do not go on hunting trips, I do not shoot deer or any other animal, I actually do not have a gun of any kind to go hunting. Many times, over the years, friends have asked me to go hunting game fowl (Guinee fowl in Africa) No thanks I do not kill birds, or any animals. My hunting days were over many years ago.

Possibly the last time I went to our farm was with Robbie Young who I met at High School. Rob and I had one pellet gun between us, I was now 16, so was Rob. Rob had the gun and there were no birds around, so he was pot shooting at different things as we walked along a path down to the river. The farm staff would milk the cows every day and bring us fresh milk and fresh cream off the top of the milk. Yummy. I did not realize this but rob hit the milk sieve 2-3 times dead center so there was a good-sized hole in the famous milk sieve. OH, geez Rob that is going to cause all kinds of goo-goo. Andy you have to say you did it, as he did not want to be chastised, by my parents, or my grand-parents. They would not have done anything to him. OH boy OK so I said I shot the milk sieve because I was bored, and the incident was over.

I did see a flock of birds that settled in one of the trees on our farm and I had never seen these birds before, I knew they were bee-eaters because we had bee-eaters in Durban. I looked through bird books of the time and no such bird was in the bird books. Many years later I found them in the South African bird book and it is called The Carmine Bee-Eater. The shooting of various birds made me want to keep them in cages, so over the next few years I collected birds trapped them and kept them in large cages.

In 1953 My dad took me up in SUNDERLAND SEA PLANE that took off from the Durban Harbor and this was to be their last ride before being placed in mothballs, never to fly again. AN aero plane that takes off from water makes a sound you have never heard before and as the plane lifts off the surface of the water, that loud sound is gone, we flew around and coming into land on water again, now this sound was three times louder than take off and we slowed to a stop. I am unable to remember more of the last sea plane ride, but the plane inside seemed bare, maybe that added to the sound as well. I was ten at the time.

Gay chasing young boys:

I am sure every little boy has been chased by gays over the years of their young lives. This happened around fourteen to sixteen years old living at Natal Command on the Snell Parade, which was and is a famous road on the beach front of Durban. Every person living in Durban knows this famous land mark. It is the military center of Natal and has subsequently been demolished. When Natal Command was built, this was far outside of town. As time moved ahead and the population grew, the city on the beach front road grew closer and closer. Between the road and the beach was a no mans' land; a special grass and small thick trees held beach sand on the beach. These low thick bushes possibly are between forty and sixty feet wide and running some four miles to the Umgeni River mouth. This thick section of hardy beach growth is a natural buffer between the beach and the rest of the land, it stops wind pushing beach sand further inland, so it is normally a *natura*l protected *zone.* This natural low thick wild growth is also home to owls and birds normally never seen anywhere else. Outside of the Natal Command (fenced-off Army grounds) is more bush but of a different kind, many four-hundred-year-old trees and kind of a bushy Savannah area. another location for various birds and those large blue-headed iguanas, noted in Natal coastlands. Between these two different bushy areas was a two-lane highway into our town and a two-lane highway out of town, called the Snell Parade, or the Marine Parade. One day after school I had taken my sling-shot to hunt for birds and those blue headed lizards. I had crossed the highway and did see a car further down the road parked, unusual; but no concern. I walked into the winding path through the thick undergrowth and a man looked like he was reliving himself just off a fork in the path. We both saw each other at the same time, and he started to say something to me. I took the opposite fork in the path and made haste to the outside on the beach. I ran towards Natal Command for thirty paces, then took another path back into the same bush, but further down, I ran through the no-mans' land and across all the traffic lanes and stood on the opposite side of the road. I was right the man had followed me through the bush and was standing closer to his car. He saw me cross the road, so he jumped into his car, as I ran into the bush on the opposite side of the road. He did a U-turn further up the highway so I ran back across the road, into the beach bush area where both of us had just left, except he was now on the opposite side of the road, I could see what he was doing and I was in control of this situation, he did a second U-Turn further down the highway and came back on the original side of the road where he had parked earlier, so I cross once again to the opposite side of the road opposite to the beach side. I was totally in control, with him in his car and me running across to the opposite of the highway, he had to continue doing U-turns, so he left. I cannot remember the words he said to me when we initially first met, but they were a little too suggestive to scare me away, plus in bush with no one to see what is going on, I would have been out of my depth had he pushed his luck. The man did four U-Turns and

I crossed the road double the time mentioned here. I mention this because it is what happened.

Soccer:

My first days of soccer the teacher had no idea what was in my mind and placed me randomly in a left half position I changed this to inside left as I wanted to score goals, not interested in defending, only scoring and for at least the first four to five soccer games never scored any goals. My dad asked me which my favorite leg to kick with, and my answer was: my right leg.

"Well, Boy, you need to get both legs ready to score."

I concentrated on my left leg as well, and the first goal ever scored was with the left leg. Yahoo, my goal-scoring career had begun. I felt sorry for all the schools who played us, we were never beaten for as long as I can remember. One Saturday Morning I heard we were going to play Addington and their big goal scorer was Kenny Honneysett, later became close friends, well into our seventy fifth birthday. I knew we were going to beat Addington, but it was my first loss, not good at all. I played under ten for school and for our club Thistle, in the Afternoon. Thistle soccer club was later bought out by Normal Elliott and changed to Durban City. Those wonderful school boy days; of soccer for school on a Saturday morning and Thistle club soccer the same afternoon were brilliant days in Durban South Africa. Our last year at Windsor Park 1958, we had Anthony Van Den Heuvel, Raymond Broad and me as the major goal scorers. I got seven goals with Anthony and Raymond both on six each. Marbles, stingers were all aggressive sports with my full confidence to win in each sport. I was always a fan of Ant van den Heuvel, he was the first person I ever saw playing cricket and a ball was hit almost out of bounds, but Anthony ran forward looking up and over his head to catch the ball. 99.999 percent of all players when catching a ball in the air run backwards with their eye on the ball, plus a glove in the catching hand. Not Anthony, he was faster running forward and looking up behind himself to catch the ball with bare hands. You try doing this! Even old professionals cannot do this. How old were we? About fourteen and fifteen years old and full of self-confidence. Raymond Broad played for one of the top professional teams when we left junior school and Ant went surfing to be-come the first South African to place Third in the world surfing championship round in Peru roughly 1965.

After living at 102 steps for a few months my dad was given a post at Natal Command and we moved to Natal Command around 1952 late in that year and we stayed at Natal Command until mid-1964 when we moved to Durban North in an Army home. During Natal Command days, I brought home owls and crows from school and they became part of the family. My mom insisted the owl had to be let go, so it was. But Joe Crow remained part of our family for many years. Living in a closed community meant there were very few children of my own age to play with, so I started my own gang and I was always the leader of my gang. Building my own gang has molded my life as well. I built a grand tree house. We would sleep in the tree house, and we would have meals in the tree house. In the afternoons I would play soccer with one of my gang. Without me knowing this was also building my character. Later in life I ran two different businesses, and both had four to five people in the business structure, where I was the M.M.W.C. (main man what counts—slang for president.) My aggressive side developed in Junior school, then the closed community made me gather followers, and this molded me for life. This was the backbone for my life, not only in sport, but also to rather set things up myself by *forming both businesses I have run over forty-five years.*

I asked my parents to send me to boarding school in 1959 so that I would have to start learning school work. I knew I had to do some learning at school, so I begged for boarding school.

High School Rugby, 1959-1961:

My parents also knew I needed to learn so boarding school it was. Billy Barker had also moved from Windsor Park to Escourt High School, so I followed. Billy was in the first team, as scrum half and

I in the team below him, also scrum half. Billy was also a drummer in the Escourt High School cadet band and the next years so was I.

At 132 pounds I was by far the smallest 5 foot, 5 inches, player on all teams I played, but I felt the most valuable of all. My first few rugby matches were a learning curve, plus our kicker was disgusting. He kept missing the poles and from soccer I knew I would get every kick over the poles. The captain kept saying "Andrew shut up we have got our kicker" and would not listen to me, the small up start. I became so frustrated that when our kicker was walking back to take his such an important kick, I ran onto the field behind his back. I passed him and kicked the ball easily over the poles to score points. From that point onwards, I was always my team's kicker, plus scrum half. As I was leaving high school the first team coach asked me to play for the first team and also be the kicker, but I could not tell him I was not planning to be at school after standard eight (standard ten in America).

One incident happened twice during a rugby game, one of the props was 280 pounds and I was on the ground possibly from getting the ball out of the scrum to the first center. When doing this, the scrum half dives with both feet high in the air, so the opposite team run into his studs of his boots. I felt a large hand grab my shorts and I was in the air legs and, arms flailing; or grabbing air, put me down, put me down. The entire school was looking and laughing.

"Come on Andy lets go," and after 20 yards puts me back on the ground. This man had picked me up with one hand and was running with me, and there was nothing I could do about this.

Then one week-end Billy Barker (first team and me in second team) played Newcastle High at Newcastle. The first team were shouting for us to win, when out of the blue this 280-pound prop got a runaway and he would have made a try. I happened to be on the opposite side of the field and I was the only obstacle in his way to scoring. Billy Barker was watching, I could not let him down, I had to take down this giant of a man. If I tackled him, he would just shove me off with one hand and his body momentum. This tackle had to be man down, because everyone was watching, so I ran at him perpendicular and would hit him side on. I decided to throw both my legs at his knees and take out his legs, with my legs. This is totally illegal; but my mind was made. My attack was opposite to what normally happens and luckily for him, I hit his right knee coming up with my thigh and swept both his legs away, and he stopped dead in his tracks. I had saved that day. Kids do not think, as I did, this is totally illegal. Had I hit his right leg after just touching the ground to take his weight, his leg would be broken. No foul was called the game went on like normal. Big proud moment for me.

Late in standard eight (Americans grade ten), I was asked to pay for the first team and to kick for the first team the following year. I had other plans for 1962.

I really loved rugby, but only played three years of rugby and never again.

The fun aspect of boarding school was a Sunday we were allowed to go out the whole day; on a ramble. The first ramble I ever went on were with Michael Kerr, Brian Chamberlain and Cedric Spencer. We went to Jones Valley and it was to be the only time we went to Jane's Valley. I was simply following. We were walking along a ledge forty feet off the ground high in the air of a cliff face and the three-inch diameter root I held on to crumbled like powder in my hand. This root must have died thirty years back with nothing inside so when I grabbed it, it simply disintegrated in my hand. Wow, that was old. This was to come and haunt me in later rambles. Michael Kerr had found a platform some forty-five feet above a stagnant pool in the river. Michael wanted to test the depth of the water below, so her threw a large rock into the dark brown water and it made a large splash. That is a sign of depth, we remained apprehensive, so he threw a second large rock into that pool and again a great big healthy splash. I am going to dive into the pool, so I stood by and watched. Michael Kerr was a fat boy and all of us were sixteen or seventeen years old at the time. Michael had convinced himself that this pool was deep, so off he went diving into this pool. He hit the water hands first and did a belly flop as his body never went under water and he stood up. The water was eighteen inches deep, on a rock-solid slimy bottom. I automatically cracked up laughing but no one else was laughing. I could not help it he was fine with scratches on his arms and chest. He was not bruised; or did not show it, just light scratches to his arms and chest. None of us followed his lead. We completed our first ramble ate our food and walked back to school. Michael Kerr was one lucky man and so were we.

Rambles lead to collecting birds and bird eggs, and I found a lifelong pal in Robbie Young, Robbie and I did everything together. One Sunday I went on a ramble with Roger Fugel, who was to die falling seven thousand feet in the Andes Mountains eight years after completing high school and he was climbing with our headmaster R.O. Pearce, also a mountaineer. On this ramble, Roger and I had found a five-hundred-foot-high cliff face and he saw cape ravens high on the cliff face, so he looked for a way to get to their nest and I would go to the top above their nest and try to see if I could find a way down to the raven's nest. There were two dead cows on the foot of this cliff, so they had obviously fallen from the top to their death. I got around to the top of the cliff above Roger, as I got close to the edge but there was a forty five degree sandy slope at the very top of the cliff, so I tried to look over and my foot slipped dragging me over the top of the cliff face, just like the cows were and I was sliding too fast to stop. Right at the very edge of this huge cliff was a root I could grab, if the root was dead (like the first one in Jones' Valley) then I was going over the cliff just like the two cows. I grabbed that root, and it was firm, but my entire body went over the cliff face, which means both hands were locked on the two-inch-thick root, so the box of bird eggs I had fell five hundred feet below me. I shouted to Roger to come and get me because I was hanging over the edge of the cliff face legs dangling. "Roger watch out for the sliding soil, it is like small beads."

The dead cows below had been caught in that same trap as I was in. Roger got a long branch and held it down to me and I climbed up the branch to him. Roger was pissed I let the eggs fall down the cliff face. We made our way back to school looking for more birds' eggs.

One day the vice principle of our school noticed I had a baby emerald cuckoo I was rearing, and he asked me if I would like a room to keep birds in and I said yes. From that point, all the guys at high school who also wanted to keep birds simply asked me if they could also join me, and soon that room was full of birds and cages. We had blue birds, red birds, black crows and pied crows, cuckoo's, hawks, owls and one Vaal Berg eagle. The Vaal Berg eagle did not last too long as it needed a rabbit every day, so it was given to the park ranges. This eagle was also a protected bird. I had started a trend that lasted all the days I was at that high school.

One of my most memorial Rambles was with Robbie Young. We were walking across a six-inch-deep river that had thirty small bull rush islands, dotted within this river, and as we were starting to walk past one little island, I saw a movement (the head of a mother wild duck dipping her head). We were on our way past her and I bluffed I did not see that small movement, but as I got in line with this little island. I dove to my right, arms spread wide and caught a mommy wild duck in my hands. I pulled one colored feather from her wing and let her go, she flew so far away she disappeared into the blue sky. We took one egg and carried on across the river. This happened again with a robin also sitting on her nest in a run-down ruin we were walking past, she ducked her head and my glance caught that small movement, and I knew it was a bird on her nest. My eyes remained in front of me, as I got within arm's length, I shot out my right arm and caught her on her nest. I let her go took one egg as well as a cuckoo's egg, then Rob and I went our way. Geez, only Andrew Buys can do this, he used to say.

One week-end I was asked to stay with a friend at their farm. His mother was a teacher at our school, Mrs. Greyling. My pal would die in a car crash five years after high school. One early morning I woke up on this farm long before everyone else, I walked around looking at the farm and noticed a gorgeous lake with bulrushes on one side and a corrugated canoe on land, between these bulrushes. I slid the canoe into the dead-calm ice-cold water and got into the canoe, then with my hands paddled out into the dam. Oops, I realized that ice-cold water was creeping up along my legs and butt area, so we were sinking. My canoe and I were slowly about to sink in this very cold mountain water. I started to turn the canoe around when two feet above the water swimming perpendicular directly at me was a large black mamba snake. Just before the snake got to my canoe, it dove under my canoe and disappeared. Well, *no way were my hands* going to go back into that water. A very big problem surfaced, my canoe was sinking, and it was filling up with even more water, so my hands went into the water to turn around and head for the shore. As I got to the shore, the canoe sunk. The nose was on land, but the rest of the canoe was well underwater.

And I got wet up to my waist. I was now out of the water and back on dry land. A snake that can swim through water with its head so high out of the water, had to be 10 feet long, and it was a bad snake. I guess these are fun boarding school days?

Being totally dedicated to your sport means you get mentally and physically stronger. This strength stops cancer and other sicknesses, you simply have zero time to be sick, you have to be at the game. It also gets your mind stronger trying to work out new ways to gets things done, how to win.

Roger Fugel:

Roger was a pal of mine who was a wiry adventure seeking junkie, just the best gent to be around, you better keep up with him, or get left behind in his dust. During one school holiday I was with Roger and we were looking for bird eggs. We were walking through a very thick mango plantation south of Durban and Roger was in front of me, but I could not see him. This has only happened once to me in my entire life and even now I wonder why I did this. We were in the shade of these thick mango trees walking in six to eight inches of weeds and grass when something told me to hold the branch above my head, and not put your right foot down. I held the branch just above my head and did not put my foot on the ground; we were in a very small path. Looking down where my foot was about to strike the ground was a large Gaboon viper (thick well-marked snake in the small path;) it was also short for its girth and very well marked. I would have put my foot on this snake had I put my foot down. I watched the snake and it moved off fast to the top of a grassy five-foot-high bank, and I saw the tail fall down the top of the bank to the floor five feet below. I knew the snake had flopped down into the grass below the red-sand bank. When cutting a dirt road on a small slope, there is normally a small perpendicular bank on one side and a soft sloping bank on the opposite side of the new road. The snake had fallen in four-inch-high grass on the side of the road just below this five-foot high red sand-bank. I jumped down called Roger and told him a Gaboon adder had fallen into this small section of grass. We got sticks and hit the grass, but it was impossible to find the snake there. Thirty years later I worked out how the snake had fooled us. I did see the tail fall over the bank, but what transpired was; that the snake went over the edge and then slid back into the grass overhang at the top of the bank, so the tail did fall over the small cliff as I had seen, but the entire snake had remained at the top of the bank and when the tail went over the edge, it was just part of the tail that flopped over; but followed the rest of the snake under that overhang on top of the bank. The snake did not fall the five feet to the bottom, it just looked like it did. That is why we did not find the snake; the snake was in the grass at the top of the bank. That part of the tail falling is all I saw, it just appeared to fall over the bank. Keep in mind I was standing on top of the bank and back a few yards.

During this same day, Roger climbed a ninety feet fir tree the ones that grow straight up ninety feet and has branches out all along the tree. This is a good nesting place for large birds like crows, owls, and hawks. I was below Roger, who was six feet above me and I was easily seventy feet up, possibly higher when I must have pulled myself up on a young branch and the entire branch (not a dead branch) pulled out of **the** socket; the branch did not break, it just pulled out of the socket, of the trees main stem. I have just realized, 50 years later, that Roger's foot may have cracked this branch along her socket line, and my new weight made the branch pull out of that socket. My body was thrust out away from the main trunk of the tree. If the branch broke, I would have fallen straight down, but pulling out of the socket made my body push out-wards away from the tree. I spread my arms hoping to break or stop my fall and fell all the way to the hard ground. I woke up in hospital with seven broken ribs. One had pierced my lung and kidney, so I was not in a good way, but soon went home and back to boarding school.

Roger as I have said before, passed away in the Andes Mountain years later, after falling seven thousand feet. R-I-P. my dear pal.

Another Roger story. Roger and I were on a Sunday ramble looking for bird eggs again and we came up on this huge tree. The girth of her base was seven feet in diameter, it went straight up with no small branches all the way up to thirty feet, then all the branches spread out in all directions, right in the middle was a super large nest, so we had come upon a hawk's, or eagle's nest that was impossible to get to. Roger looked around and found a young wattle tree that had grown up close to one of the branches and Roger's plan was to climb the wattle tree, then when the wattle tree bent over, he would direct it to the branch of this large tree with the nest inside. Up went Roger and the wattle tree started to bend. He went higher and the wattle bends more, but the bend was missing the direction he was after, so he placed his weight a little to the right, the wattle tree then touched that branch. It was now getting tricky because the wattle tree is starting to get thin at that height Roger was at, but Roger pushed his luck and inched up a little higher. Now Roger was close to the big trees branch, and just a little more and Roger touched the branch. One more inch, Roger let go of the wattle tree and grabbed the big tree's branch with both hands and his body swung under the branch, then his legs gripped the branch and he eased around and on top of the branch. Okay this was great. The wattle tree sprung far away again. Roger shouts, "I can see two baby chicks and they are hawks." Roger climbs onto the large nest and had both baby birds in his hands. "Okay Andy let me work out how to get the birds down to you without hurting them and let me work out how to get down." Oh, dear, I could not reach the wattle tree from here and I could not drop down thirty feet to the ground. Roger was totally stuck. "Andy, go and get my brother Alan and have Alan bring some rope so I can get down." OK I rushed back to our school which is seven miles away and I had to find Alan Fugel. I do find Alan and explain the situation, but I was worried Alan will not find the tree where Roger was stuck. However, Alan took enough rope and went to get his brother down. Both arrived back at school when it was very dark, but all okay as I explained the details to the master in charge.

Oh Dear Me:

For one reason or another my dad let me go home from high school by train one semester. The train took over night and cost nothing compared to traveling two hours from Durban (my hometown) to Escourt and another two hours back to Durban by the sea. A few of us boys board the train at 5.00 p.m. and we would be home at 7 a.m. the next day. In our compartment of the train we had one gentleman around the age of thirty-two years old with us and he was such a charming, friendly man. He bought us kids a few beers and asked us to please remind him to get off the train at North Port; his wife will be there waiting for him. You guys would easily recognize North Port because the buildings were yellow brick with red tile roof, but it was the yellow you will see at **10 p.m. at** night that stood out. All other buildings along the way were a dull red, except for South Port, I was to find out later South Port is also yellow and South Port is first stop, the next was North Port, some ten miles further down the line. As time went by during this evening, he ended up drinking in the bar area of the train. At 10;45 p.m. that night our train was just pulling away from a yellow brick building and I knew he was still drinking in the bar, so I picked up his suitcase and ran to the bar, by this time the train had gained momentum and those yellow buildings were flashing past. I handed him his suitcase and said, "This is your station. "His face changed and for a second he held his suite-case, and I left him sitting at the stool I made my way back to my compartment. On the way I looked back out the window and saw the nice gentleman take a large step out the train suitcase in hand, the train was easily doing forty miles per hour and we were near the end of the station. This was a long huge step onto the passing platform and that station floor was going past very fast, as his foot hit the station platform his foot dragged his leg sideways in the biggest step he had ever taken in his life. His leg was pulled twenty feet back, his body spun, and he and his suitcase hit the concrete sidewalk spinning, and the suitcase opened, spewing clothes into the air looked like a balloon expelling air all at once. I felt the gentleman's pain. I had no idea what to do next. I told the pals in my cabin what just happened. We will tell the next station master, so we waited until the next station arrived. We did not have to wait long as it soon appeared. It was North Port and the buildings were yellow brick. As the train came to a halt, I jumped off the train knowing I had little time before the train pulled away again. I found the office manager's office, and he was sitting at his desk. "Sir, Mr. Barnard stepped off the train at South Port and must be hurt. His wife is waiting here somewhere for him. Can you find Mrs. Barnard and tell her to drive to South Port to get her husband?" I had looked at the entire station and did not see one solitary soul anywhere. That is all I said, then ran back to the train as it started to pull away from the station. Oh geez, I talked that nice man into stepping off the train at high speed, and it was the wrong station. Geez, I put my foot in it sometimes; this time someone got really badly hurt. Sorry Sir, I never saw, or heard about that again, I hope his wife found him.

School band:

I started drums as I wanted to be in the school band, just like Billy Barker, so did Robbie Young. I got into the school band and was a drummer for three years coming third behind the same two gentlemen for the last two years in the band as <u>northern Natal's best 3 drummers</u>. For the first time in history Escourt High School was Natal's top school cadet band in 1961 and the small town had us parade up and down the ***main street.***

In a nutshell, I had mastered soccer, and rugby, and our school band had won the best cadet band in all the state of Natal. My life as an army brat had led me to pick my own small group of friends. Now it was time to start work.

Starting work:
Business and Climbing the Ladder of Life: March 3, 1962.

Okay, let's commence with my first day of work after I left high school: This is covered in great detail in the business side of this book, because we have now started the serious side of sports. I started and completed work in 1962 as a learning draftsman in the post office, drawing plans for telephone cables underground.

Day 1 of Army Training:

Let me start from the beginning of Army training. On March 3, 1963, I was nineteen years of age and 132 pounds and 5 foot 5 inches tall.

The first day you get your hair shaved off, plus you are issued with all your Army clothes, shorts, overalls, shirts, jackets, longs, socks, boots, and two pairs of tackies (tennis shoes). Nothing fitted this little man. Everything was three and four sizes too large for me. Tough, wear them. My shoe size was an eight and the tackies (tennis shoes) fifteen, so they were never worn.

MARCHING:

Now the parading starts 8.00 a.m. to 10.00 a.m. fifteen minutes smoke break, then 10;15 a.m. to noon lunch at 12;30-1;30 p.m. lectures on supply and transport, until 3.00 p.m. fifteen-minute smoke break, then to lectures to 5.00 p.m. meet for dinner 6-7 p.m.

Okay so I knew that I would be picked on by the drill master who was a real bad angry man. He seemed angry with someone all the time. We had not been going long when he called halt. Walked up to me and shouted in my ear. "What is your name slug?" "My name, sir, is Page."

"Yah Page, I got your number the very first day." and he went on to lather me with insults. That first day came and went, and so did day 2, then on day 3 during parade, I heard, Page, while we were marching, "Company halt." Here it comes, that swearing loud-moth in my ear.

"Page are you deaf?" I did not answer.

"Page I am speaking to you." "Sir I am not Page; my name is Andrew Buys."

You could hear the Eiffel Tower vibrate and start to fall in France. "You are not Page?" "No, sir, my name is Buys."

"Ok, in a quiet voice, company march. Hip two-three-four, hip-two-three-four."

No more issues with Dog Face. Dog Face got his nick name from the guys in our platoon. I have seen men of twenty-four years of age; cry with the permanent force sergeants shouting, plenty of adjectives, in their ear.

Mark Krog:

Mark and I were a naughty combination, we did not smoke, but everyone else did. Walking into a lecture at 8.00 a.m. everyone took off their Army hats and hung them on the wall at the back of the lecture room, on hooks. We would all remember which hook our hats hung from. At lectures there would be a smoke break at 10.00 a.m. to 10.15.a.m. While everyone was outside smoking, Mark and I would take forty hats and switch them around on different hooks, as well as, invert the brass Army badge on each hat, then sheepishly go outside for a few minutes. Pandemonium had been created, but no one had noticed, until we were told to assemble outside for lunch later. Lectures resumed immediately. The lecture ended at 12.30pm for lunch and everyone would rush to grab their hats and then assemble outside and stand in formation in the bright sunshine. Only Mark and I were outside with the permanent force sergeant, the three of us waiting, and waiting for the rest of the bunch. The sergeant would get angry and go back shouting at the forty men looking for their hats. The shouting did not help matters. Slowly the men started to form up, as each person found their hat. The Sergeant by now was livered and started to pick on a few late commers. Out of the blue the Sergeant noticed one man with an upside-down badge on his hat.

Oh, now the four-letter words were spewing out of his mouth, Mark and I just broke down, we made a few of our pals irritated with us.

Away with Out Leave;

    At your first lecture we are told not to leave the base for the first six weeks under *any* circumstance, if you wanted a week-end pass, you had to ask for it, only after the first 6 weeks, were complete. If anyone was caught away without leave, then he will go straight to detention barracks, the military police will pick you up and take you to jail. In detention barracks (military jail), you must march while doing your daily tummy movements. I had made pals with Peter Reid. Peter told me there was a wonderful party on at a castle in Pretoria, so I said to Peter.

    "This is the perfect time to AWOL, no one thinks we will do it, so get some civilian clothes and have one of your pals pick us up outside the camp on Saturday evening early." Peter and I jumped the fence and we were back partying, that was some serious party. During the party we were told of a second party the following Saturday, so we set up doing this again. The second week-end arrived and we went AWOL once again. We were in one barrack with sixty other new boys, there were eight other such barracks. After the second week-end partying with the girls, I said to Peter too many other troops in our Bungalow were also planning to go AWOL on the third Saturday, so I said we would not go. Sure, as rain falls from heaven, three guys were caught and sent to detention barracks. Peter wanted to go on the fourth Saturday, I said no Pete, but he persisted, so we went and came back into the arms of Dog Face. Now I got you, Buys and Reid, you are going to D.B. Dog Face made a report that gets sent to the military police and then the military police come and pick you up and take you to jail. In this short time, I bumped into Gerald Ensor Smith who was a very big pal of my dad's, I told Gerald what had transpired. Meeting Gerald was such a coincidence. Gerald had come to the same place to study for a higher rank, I had no idea he was here. I just happened bumped into him.

Gerald told me not to say anymore and he would get back to me. Four hours later Gerald got back to Peter and me and told us, "If anyone asked, just to say the military police had told us to get our tooth brush and one towel ready for five p.m. that day." He said the day would pass and the following day would also pass. Just say to anyone who asks you, "The military police were going to pick you up at noon the next day."

Now Gerald gave us the background. Gerald said that Dog Face had to charge us within twenty-four hours, which he had done. If twenty-four hours passed and he did not charge us, then he was not allowed to. Gerald Ensor-Smith had torn out the entire charge page and burned it. If dog face felt the military police were going to pick us up, he had no reason to doubt that we would be picked up by the police. That twenty-four hours came and went, and both Peter Reid and I never went to detention barracks. I never heard from Dog Face again. "Oh, thank you Gerald."

Army Soccer:

Every Saturday after this, I played soccer for the Defense Senior Team and they were far more talented than I had expected. This team represented all air force, all army, supply staff as well as military, so there are some one thousand people to select from. I was always a striker and always got goals. On a Saturday I would go and pick up my own allocated car a 1950 Ford and head for various soccer fields in and around Pretoria and Johannesburg. Every Saturday I got out of Diensfak Skool (Services School). We were playing somewhere, and I did hear that the selectors of the Transvaal soccer board would be at this one game looking for talent to be in the Northern Transvaal team to play the South African University team. I scored one of the most spectacular goals I ever scored during that match. To me, in rugby; or soccer, size meant zero. I was always super confident, was also faster than 95 percent of all of them, and also had longevity on my side when it came to soccer.

The ball was high in the air coming down fast, my aim was to hit the ball before it hit the ground. Two defenders were almost on me and they planned to hit me as the ball hit the ground. One foot from the ground, I hit the ball and the kick also gave the ball a dip, it looked like it may go over the crossbar, but it dipped in and the three of us were on the ground in a heap. I knew the ball went into the back of the net. Now that was a humdinger. The three of us were on the ground in our own ball of humans, but I knew the ball was in. Two of our team were selected to play for Northern Transvaal against South African University, our full back and myself. State colors for Soccer.

The sportsman side of my life was wide awake and well. We did play SA university and we lost one goal to our no goals. I did have two very good shots at goal during the match, but no goals scored. After the first three months of army training, everyone gets moved and I went to sixteen supply and transport where I got rank for the soccer achievement. The Major said not one of his boys had ever made the northern Transvaal team in all the years he had run sixteen supply and transport. Our team Trainer said to me if he had eleven Andrew Buys', we would beat every team in the world. Thank you, sir.

The final three months I got to stay at home in my own bed and finish my army training at Natal Command with Eddy Bigham and Robert Embelton. Posts were made for all three of us in Natal Command.

After Our First 9 Months of Basic Training:

For the next three years we had also to do three weeks, each year, training in the Army. Three things happened during these times that need a note. All of us would be in the bush living in tents with ice every morning and we would do Army maneuvers. This one time we were told the enemy was ahead of us and each one of us had to dive into a bush and make ourselves small. I selected a bush and dived in face first. I was in so deep inside this small bush my face was almost against the stem of this small bush, and this head rose level with my eyes three inches away from my face. It was a puff-adder. Slowly I moved away back out of the bush and let that snake be. Well we are in the darkest Africa, where you find the largest, most venomous snakes around.

One night we were going to do a full-on maneuver with bombs and blanks going off and one team had to catch the other. I had lost Sergeant Warby so I climber a hill and shouted across the valley. "Sergeant Waaarby, I'm lost. Sergeant Waaaaarby I'm lost." A few minutes later Sergeant Warby appeared. "Shut up Buys, for God's sake." I thought it was funny. It is something I should never have done with my Dad in the army in Durban, that must have irritated the majors running the show, far below.

One day everyone was placed in four covered transport trucks and we had to wear tackies (tennis shoes) as we were going to be placed some fifteen miles away from camp and we were going to have to find our own way back to camp. I did not think I had to do the run because I had rank. Oh no, Buys, you run as well, so I was last to get out for the four trucks. I walked to the bank of the river and saw a Hammerkop nest in a large willow tree. This is normally where owls roost, so up the tree I went, it takes some time to open such a huge nest because the roof is done with thick sticks and mud to keep warm inside. Plus, snakes love these nests as well, so when opening a Hammerkop nest watch out for snakes. There was nothing inside, so I closed it up as best I could, then got down the Willow tree and started to follow the path up a very high mountain. I ran past all the walkers soon and crested a high hill, only to find more hills with a long line of Army guys running as best they could. I soon ran past all of them then crested another hill and ran down a long dip at full speed peeling off runners by the dozen. I had seemed to get a second wind and went over the next ridge easily also to run down to a fence before a dirt road and hung a right onto the dirt road now there were few runners in front of me and I picked all of them off easily. Around a long curve with one more dude ahead of me I went past him easily and into the camp in third position. No one would have beaten me had I got to the task of running and not climbing a willow tree, looking for owls, all that after getting out last of the four trucks.

SPORT: IS THE BACKBONE TO BUSINESS

Army Standing Guard:

The second night March 1963 that we were in the Army we were all called into the major hall of Diensfak-Skool (Services School) in Robert's Heights. The day before we had all be given boots clothes and overalls that were too big for us and our modern F1. This is a gun like the ones the soldiers get given when going to war. They can be placed on automatic firing many rounds per minute or shooting one single bullet and we were told to sleep with our guns, to love our guns; and never to be seen without our guns. We were told to meet with our uniform and guns at the hall at the double. The colonel spoke to us saying there was a POQO scare, and we would all be sent to various delicate locations to protect them. We were loaded into trucks and taken to our location to protect and one gentleman who was with me was Robert Embelton, a man I remain very close with today. We arrived and found one permanent force sergeant in the control room waiting for us. He allocated guard duty to us and so the night began. The first night we stood guard and I was to stand guard 12.00 a.m. and 2.00 am. After a small super, I put my head down for sleep and was woken by the gentleman who stood guard before me. I knew where to go and what I was supposed to guard. This area was well lit up at night but there were spots here and there you could not see. We must have been on the outskirts of Pretoria where it is not built up at that time. I did not want to stand next to a tree as I would be silhouetted if there were any enemy outside and I would be a prime target. I did not want anyone to be in any position to see me. I wanted to be the sole eyes controlling this quiet, dead-of-night section I was instructed to cover. This night it was dead quiet, you would hear a small twig crack in the night if it were stood on. I selected a small three possible twenty-five feet high, which was reasonably dark inside, and I climbed up into the firm branches. I was 10 feet off the ground and sat quietly, watching and listening. My view was 360 Degrees, and no one could see me, I had a very quiet uneventful guard period. Then from the tree, I heard my relief gentleman softly call my name. "Andy, where are you?" As he was slowly walking toward me, not knowing where I was. Oh, we were issued with twenty-five rounds, which were kept in our pocket. To slide one round into this new modern automatic it had a short leaver action which went something like a loud metal to metal clicking sound. That sound at the dead of night can be heard for miles around especially if you want that sound to be heard, you do it hard and firm and it makes a noise, which is very unmistakable, even for a person who has never heard that sound before. YOU know a serious gun is being loaded. I loaded the gun without placing a bullet into the breach, I just did the action. My relief could not see me but stopped dead in his tracks.

"Andy, geez it's me Harold your relief."

I waited 2 seconds and said, "I know Harold, keep walking I am at the tree." "I cannot see you." He said as he walked towards the tree. "Where are you, Andy?"

I am up the tree above you, and it was so dark he could not see me. "You bugger, I thought you were going to pull the trigger." Thanks Harold. It was my turn to sleep the rest of the night.

The following day we all stood guard again, this time I was told to walk the entire grounds and to check all buildings and fences, which I did, and this time Robert Embelton was with me. Anyway, we were walking near some low shrubbery and out hopped a rabbit, so I put one live round into my gun and aimed and shot at the rabbit. The shot went high and the rabbit hopped away. The noise of the gun going off was like a huge cannon blast that rang in your ears for thirty seconds. Andy you are crazy to have shot the gun the sergeant had told us not to, unless it was life or death. "Okay Robert, lets walk back to the control room and let me tell the Sergeant what happened."

I walked in and the sergeant already knew a shot went off. "What happened?" I heard the bush rattle and asked, "who goes there?" No answer. I did that again and asked, "Who is this?" Nothing I saw a flash and I shot. It was a rabbit, but the gun sights are set on two hundred yards and I was very close to the rabbit, the shot went over it's head. The shot missed. "Geez, Buys, I now have to make a report explaining how one round is missing." A few times during my training at services school I had three permanent force officers ask me if it was me who shot at the rabbit. Yes, a little bit naughty, but good to hear that gun. I never heard about this again and never saw that same sergeant again. I do not think he got into any trouble anyway.

November 22, 1963:

In the army, November 22, 1963 I was in Army uniform on our home verandah (the front porch) at Natal Command when my dad (sergeant major) came into view walking home from his office to say JFK had been assassinated. We were all shocked to our bones.

Surfing:

On January 1, 1964 I took one month off after Army duty and started surfing. I bought a second-hand, light green-and-white Anglia and started surfing. It was a tough sport to master but did not take me long with persistence plus Robbie Young and all my other buddies Kenny Honneysett, Max Wetland, Denny Wilson, Bruce Morgan, Ant van den Heuvel, and Anthony Morris were all surfing so how could I not master this one? After a week every day, I was up and riding waves. Planning to be surfing up to the age of sixty years old. To advertise the first Gunston 500 surfing competition my picture was large in the newspaper. And I did take part in the very first Gunston 500 at North Beach in 1964 or 1965.

September 1964: Endless Summer:

As a surfer in 1964 to 1967, I had been one of the first Durban surfers to travel down to St Francis Bay in September of 1964 to surf Jefferies Bay, after the movie was filmed there by Mr. Bruce Brown. We had heard of Bruce Brown making a movie and he loved Jefferies Bay waves, so did we. One incident stands out in my mind from September 1964. The four of us had traveled from Durban to St, Francis Bay and we stayed in a small thatched building, on the beach. Once night at 3.00 a.m. I heard the loudest bang, just like a movie. This was a bang that ripped out my heart. My brain told me a bomb from World War 11 had hit our little cottage square on. Gingerly we switched on the light. Clouds of dusty smoke were starting to settle, our room was full of dust, our door of our bedroom to the main lounge was smashed by bricks, rocketing through the door. Those bricks went right through our door. The lounge was covered in Bricks and the chimney demolished. Lightning had hit the chimney and spat the bricks in all directions, but most had hit the bedroom door. The guy staying in the bunk bed above me was older than me, and I at the time was twenty years old. I jumped into bed with him I had got such a fright and said. "I don't care what the guys think, but I am here to stay the rest of the night." He did not argue. The next morning, we had breakfast called the caretaker explained the incident, then hit the surf. That was also the first time I saw dolphins surfing in and on the waves.

When a Small Child Is Killed in Front of You:

In the middle of January 1965, I parked my car in point Road Durban. I was on my way to pick up a girl and go to badminton. I walked along the lit pavement at 7.00 p.m. near shops in Point Road. A man and his wife were walking towards me going west on Point Road towards West Street. I was walking east. Twelve feet in front of them was their three-year-old child taking in everything, when suddenly the child turned left and ran between two parked cars into the dark road. The child was in the middle of the road and was hit full on, by an unsuspecting car. The kid flew high in the air and yards away. The mother was screaming at the top of her voice and picked up the child, all three jumped into the same car and sped off to Addington-Hospital around the block. I never knew what happened to the child, but at a ninety percent guess, she, or he passed away, almost immediately. Only when I was seventy years old did I work out why the child did what it did. This traffic incident always worried me. Why did the child suddenly turn at right angles and run fast between the two parked cars and into the oncoming traffic?

The child's height is only three feet, and he/she was standing on the lit pavement – If a three-foot person is standing on a lit pavement and you happen to be next to a gap between two parked cars. The road at 7.00 p.m. is black between each car. Now if three cars on the opposite side of the road flash past, the child would see six red taillights flash right in his/her face. That is what attracted this small three old child, the flashing taillights of the cars on the other side of the road. To the child he/she sees red flashing lights in quick succession, so he/she wants to see what all the flashing red lights were all about. The child turns at right angles and runs towards the flashing lights. This happened when I was twenty-one years old and it took me fifty years to work that out. Flicking red lights, no one could have projected that that would happen.

Jimmy Reese:

Back to surfing, what a grand sport. Laying on the beach one day with Jimmy Reece, soaking up the sun, we were around twenty years old, when Jimmy's little brother ran up to us in a serious panic. "Jimmy, Jimmy" – "Okay brother, spit it out." "I do not know what to do, I am so deep in the goo-goo." "Spit it out boet (slang for brother)," "I found out that Carol is pregnant." Both Jimmy and I cracked up laughing out loud. "No Andy and Jimmy, don't play games I have no idea what to do." We remained laughing when he blurted out, that Pamela was also pregnant. Well, this little seventeen-year-old has two girls; pregnant, both at the same time. My tummy was sore from laughing, and Jimmy was also in a ball cracking up laughing. Jimmy eventually sorted that out. I cannot remember what transpired. Jimmy had another story waiting for me. The newspapers were full of Leith Jardine counterfeiting American dollars and I remember seeing Leith riding around Durban in a Pontiac GTO in 1965 or 1966. The police picked up Leith regarding counterfeiting. Leith was a printer working at Brown Davis and Platt and Jimmy Reese was Leith's apprentice. Leith had instructed Jimmy to work overtime and print fake American twenty-dollar bills. Leith and his wife would take a trip to the USA and wash twenty-dollar-bills for good money. Apparently, the work on the money was poor. This was told to me by Jimmy Reese after he spent three years in prison. Here is what Jimmy told me years afterwards. "I did not think twice to do what Leith had told me to do. I was the apprentice and he my boss, so the printing went on and I got overtime pay as well." A few years after Jimmy was out of prison, he told me what happened to him. One night at 4.00 a.m. Jimmy and his wife were sleeping and their front door was broken down by the SWAT Team and six men had guns, on both, who were still in bed. His wife asked, what was happening, but all that was said was MR. Reese get dressed, under our supervision and come with us. Jimmy was handcuffed. Jimmy's wife had no idea where they were taking him, so she went to the Point Road police station to ask and Jimmy was in a cell right there. Jimmy had to be the cleanest most, honest gentleman around. YES, he may have been naïve, but he is one gent who should never have gone to jail. Yes, he should have known better.

Around 1964:

After partying and drinking I took a girl (Leslie) to my favorite lover's lane spot. I had been here many times and it was late at night around 1.00 a.m. a dark night where you had to go under the Umgeni Bridge and into the open grass area, following the head lights of my dad's Ford Zephyr. The grass was about three feet high, but I was on the right path, so I thought. Suddenly the nose of my dad's car disappeared and the front of the vehicle plus both lights were under water. I could see the bright headlights about twelve inches underwater shining brightly. The lights lit up the brown muddy water for three feet and no further.

Gosh, did I panic. My Dad would kill me if I called him at two in the morning and the car had to be towed out of this remote bog. "What are you doing here and who is this lady?" I was hoping none of that would happen, so back to the real world. I went to the front of the car both headlights well underwater. I stood on the floor of the water in my shoes, I could stretch down and pull up on the front bumper. I went back to the car had the girl get into the driver's seat and put her foot on the accelerator and also the clutch. "When the car moves back take both feet off the pedals." "No, I cannot do that!"

"Yes, you can, just do what I say, and we will get out of this situation!" I had to show her how to keep the accelerator humming at one firm speed and when to let the clutch out. Once the car moves just take both feet off both pedals. She got the message and I went to the front of the car bent down and pulled the front up with all my might. "Drop the clutch!" I shouted. She did, the car moved back, one yard, but that was all I needed. By now I am totally wet with muddy shoes. I had kept my shoes on all the time. I could now reverse out and we went home. The mood had changed.

Motor-cycle Racing, 1967-1968:

This started as far back as World War 11. My dad had a pal during World War 11 who lived in Johannesburg, and starting in 1958, Charles Hammer asked my dad if his sons could stay with us because they were racing motorcycles at Roy Hesketh Circuit, or Westmead, where Gary Hocking was killed. I never saw that circuit, but we did get tickets to watch at Roy Hesketh as few times, and only the motor cycles interested me. Remember since I was three years old, I had promised my dad never to ride, or ask for a motor cycle and I kept that promise. Over the following years many different young men would stay with us during the race days and then head back to Johannesburg. In 1965, Errol Cowan and Tommy Johns started to stay with us, and both my sisters were at the boy noticing age. Dianne loved Errol's soft blue eyes, but I suggested she opt for the steady dude, Tommy, and she did. Tommy and Errol would always ask me to go to the race-track with them I said. "NO, you come and surf with me." I hit the beach and they both did their racing with my family in tow. One Saturday I was in Cape Town and both Errol and Tommy were racing I had nothing planned, so I used their two tickets to go and watch them for the very first time.

Errol won the 500-cc race, and Tommy won the 250-cc race and I was hooked. One week later I was in Johannesburg purchasing my first motor-cycle, a pucka racing 250-cc Bultaco from Errol Cowan. I had convinced Tommy that I wanted to race motorcycles, so Tommy drove me to Johannesburg to purchase Errol Cowan's

250-cc Bultaco. Errol had just returned from Europe doing all the MOTOGP rounds on his 500-cc matchless and his 250-cc Bultaco during 1996. This was a pucka racing machine and it went like hell. I walked into Errol's house in Edenvale and threw all the money in the air and said. "OK where is my new race bike?" Errol loved that. The next day Tommy and I traveled back home with the new Bultaco on a trailer. By now Tommy and my sister Diane were a couple and Tommy was her first boy-friend.

My first outing on my Bultaco was very different to all other motor-cycle-riding-people, from a bicycle to a racing bike. On a bicycle you never touched the front brake. On a race bike you use 99 percent front break. I rode around the circuit as fast as possible not using that front break at all, just like a bicycle. Half-way down the main straight that rear brake went on and it took for ages to slow down, then through the one hundred mile per hour sweep, I also jumped on that rear brake to do a huge sideways slide, but I made that corner. When I came into the pits, I said to Tommy, "Geez, it is hard to stop the bike." He could hear me sliding through the one hundred mile per hour sweep. I am twenty-six years old here, late December 1966. He told me do not touch that rear brake, and do all your breaking with your front break, and they all laughed at me. Okey-Doke. Now I was able to settle down, but my first race would be Easter week-end 1967, I had to wait three months for that first race. I had been riding the Bultaco for eight months when my grand pa passed, and my parents bought me a new TD1 C Yamaha from the factory. Tommy had ordered one, so we ordered two in late 1967. I had not done too many races so the bike was premature for me, but at the time I was pleased to have a competitive racing bike. I raced this bike until July 1968 when I retired from the sport. I had crashed far too much, breaking one collar bone and being concussed three times, plus money was very short indeed. George Roland Purchased my Yamaha TD1C.

Married Gaile, February 28, 1970:

The following is 1970 -1979, living at Sherwood, a free-standing home, on the outskirts of Durban.

I met my wife in October 1968, and we were married February 1970. My racing bike was sold in 1968 and I settled into married life, to go catching marine fish for the next three years.

An apartment with a difference.

Gaile and I were married in Durban North in February 28, 1970. After our honeymoon in the Drakensberg, we moved into an apartment in Point Road. Point Road was the local prostitute hang out and we often got woken up by hookers fighting at 3.00 a.m. below our third-floor apartment. I had never heard boys swear like an angry hooker. They would rip their blouses off and hit each other with their high-heels and their mouths spewing bad words. I had always lived in a single-family home, so apartment life to me was totally unacceptable. I started to save as much money as possible. Never listen to professionals, because here is what I was told in those days. "Andrew, do not save your money, because as fast as you can save, up goes interest rate, as well as cost of living and you will never catch up." Garbage. When you are the only dude in town with a saved $4,000, you are somebody. I had seen a piece of land I wanted to purchase, so I approached a building society and explained that I had $4,000 and wanted to purchase the land to build a home on and the gentleman said, "Deposit the money with our company and you can write them a check, making the land yours. So that is what was done. I then went back two months later and asked for a loan to build a home on the land and the same gentleman said. "Go ahead Andrew and break ground we will pay for the construction of the house and you will pay our building society seven hundred dollars per month for thirty years." So, our house in Loon Road, Sherwood Durban, was built and we moved in in late 1972.

There was one incident at this home that sticks in my mind. Behind us to our right lived a taxi driver and his hooker wife. Their porch-light was the traditional red light on the front porch. One day their little toy pom ran barking at me. The dog was very far away, so I threw a flat stone at the dog anticipating a large curve, if the flat stone was to get anywhere near the dog. The stone did a large arch and hit the pooch on the tip of his nose, knocking him out. I was shocked. The doggie rolled over and all four feet pointed to the stars. I had not expected to hit the dog, I ran in a panic to assist the fallen doggie and he was out cold. Geez, I rubbed him and spoke to him, but his eyes were glazed over, then I heard the lady calling the dog's name, and she was getting closer and closer. She had not seen me throw the stone, so as she got on top of me, the dog was coming around. I said, "He stopped barking and fell over, but he is getting better now." She picked the dog up and went back home. Oh dear, we do stupid things now and again.

Camping and Marine Fish 1970-1973:

All the sports from here forward were from me opening my own drawing office and supported 100 percent by myself and my wife, Gaile. The office was in Payne Brothers building in west street, in the center of Durban. Called Drawing Service. These were fun years with a lime green beach buggy. My big pal in those days, was Errol Kinton. I had just purchased a winch and fitted the winch to my beach buggy. Errol Kinton and I had taken a long week-end to go up the north coast to catch marine fish well past Sodwana Bay. After catching fish on a Saturday, Errol and I decided to see how well the winch worked. We were way past Sodwana Bay, and not possible anyone would be within sixty miles of us. Not one soul would ride past us for the next three weeks, it was so off the beaten track. On this afternoon we had nothing to do, so we found a soft beach to bury the beach buggy flat on the floor boards into soft sea sand. To do this I had to turn the front wheels and go back and forward until the green beach buggy was down on her floorboards into the sea sand. Now we were well and truly stuck. The next chore was to bury the spare wheel into the sea sand further away and then tie the spare wheel to the beach buggies new winch, and this was all done.

Then Errol and I sat with beer in each hand looking at the buggy with the rear tire buried behind us. Ah now let's watch this new winch pull the buggy out of the sand. I pull up the cable slack with the winch handle and beer in my other hand, and we are both facing and focused on the buggy. That rear tire is buried under the soft beach behind us. Click the line is taught and working, everything is working but there is zero movement of beach buggy. The beach buggy should be hopping out of the soft sand? Together we turn together, clicking at the same time and that spare tire is hopping towards us, happy as can be. Hop, hop, with each click of the handle of the winch. We just cracked up laughing. Laughing out loud and our tummy sore from laughing, we realized this thing is not working. We now have a very big problem. We are stuck solid and it is impossible for any human being to be within miles of where we were sitting with our bogged down lime green beach buggy. Very luckily for me there was one pointed rock close by, so I shackled the end of the winch line around the rock and pulled the buggy out. When I got back home, I found out we had to bury the tire perpendicular to the car to create surface area, not flat on the sand bottom. We never tried that one again.

More Marine Fish Fun:

Tony Hall Jones one of my dad's pals became a very good friend of mine, so one week-end I traveled with Tony in a five-jeep caravan to Cozy Bay, this is just further up the north coast of Natal and way past Sodwana Bay. The first night we stopped at Sodwana Bay at Midnight and all of us slept on the beach around our Jeeps. I always carried an ultra-light camping bed so did Tony. It was a beautiful night so all of us slept in the open Tony and I were in our sleeping bags on top of our ultralight camping bed (or stretcher). At 3.00 a.m. we heard all sorts of noises shouting and jeeps moving, and I could feel my butt getting a little wet, but I was warm, so I remained sleeping. This was the same for Tony. In the morning when I awoke, and as far as I could see was water all around us. Our jeep was close by and only Tony and I were in the same spot. Everyone else had run for high ground. The river had bust her banks, due to spring high tide. Ha, ha, we were fine. Lying in our sleeping bags and on our stretchers as far as we could see all around us was four inches of water and in the distance were the rest of the bunch on a hill. These week ends were always wonderful to experience, and we always came home with beautiful fish. The marine fish and soft coral life up the north coast of South Africa, plus Maputo or Mozambique have gorgeous fish and corals, far prettier than all the Caribbean.

1971: Around this time in life Debbie was born November 17, 1971. Gaile had come home from the doctor who told her our babe was two weeks away and I bet this was a Monday evening at 5.00 p.m. In those days we read our books before falling asleep I was woken up by Gaile saying in her very gentle voice. "Andrew, wake up, we need to go to the hospital, the babe is coming." I said, "Go to sleep it is 2 weeks away and I fell asleep again." I was woken up a second time thirty minutes later. "Andrew we must go to the hospital!" I noticed her bags were packed and on the bed. Oh, geez here we go with a false alarm, so reluctantly I got dressed and drove her to the hospital. She went in and I parked the car, and when I got back to the hospital, the nurse said. "You are lucky to have got here when you did, your little girl is born, you nearly had a birth in your car……." Then it hit me, and I walked in to see my first child. Big smile from Gaile as if to say, now how about that? Okay well done. Debbie entered the world with a bang. I made 100 percent sure when Susan was born to be at the hospital early, so as not to be stupid again. Susan took forever to arrive.

1972/1973 Marine Fish Collecting:

It was illegal to dive or snorkel in the busy Durban Harbor because a scuba diver was killed. Another large ocean liner was held up docking, because a scuba diver had gone under water and the captain did not want to harm the man in anyway, so scuba diving and snorkeling were stopped. This was done a few years before I started to keep and catch marine fish. I did sneak in a good few snorkeling trips in Durban bay to catch lemon spots, jumping beans, moorish idols and painted surgeons. There was one particular spot that I saw rainbow colored wrasse, it was to be one of only two places I had ever seen them, so I did want one for my tank at home. There was a huge issue with catching them. They were living between old cables and no matter what I did I could not catch them. They were one fish that I never ever caught, and I kept trying, but those cables were a nightmare, when it came to catch them. Anyway, one sunny Sunday afternoon, my wife and I had gone to this spot to try once again. I would pull on my wet suit, no arms and very short on the legs as the water is tropical, so not cold. On went the mask and fins and I was flipping around concentrating on how to go about outthinking these fish. My attention was drawn above the water and a man in a thirty-five-foot boat was close to me. He beckoned me to swim to him. This was the local Parks Board sheriff. He lent over the rail of the boat and said. "Jump into my boat, sir!" I did what was asked? "You know you are not allowed to snorkel in the Bay right!" "Yes sir, I know." "OK we got that right," said the Sheriff. "Take off your fins mask and wet suite." I did what was asked of me. By this time, he had motored about one hundred yards into the deep bay. Yikes, we were far from the spot where I had first got into the water.

"Mr. Buys you know how to contact the Parks Board?" "Yes, sir." "Well call them on Monday and ask for my address. My name is Joe Fletcher (I have long since forgotten his name.) They will tell you where to come to my office and make it sharp Monday at 3.00 p.m. I am not going to fine you, but if you do not appear Monday consider all your gear confiscated. Have we got each other?" "Yes sir." "Lastly do not snorkel in the bay again. If I catch you, it will be a huge fine. Thank you, Mr. Fletcher. I did meet Mr. Fletcher at his office, and he suggested I pick up all my gear and beat it. Okey-Doke. Thank you again.

Losing a Man at Sea:

I had gone up with my pals, all wanted to catch marine fish. We could do that outside of the Parks Board legal area. I had my own hard-bottomed inflatable boat and an outboard-motor, plus all scuba gear and there were three of us. My years of surfing proved valuable here because from the beach you had to first get through five feet of waves, once past that, there was a flat section of water where you had to plan to wait for a clam period to shoot through the seven to nine feet of waves, then you were free and clear. We went far past where we needed to, three miles north, then anchored the tender to rocks forty feet below and the three of us started to look for marine fish to catch. We had a great time and caught a few nice fish. The three of us all remained together and came up the anchoring together, so all was good. All of us had catch boxes to keep the fish alive in plus and extra tank in the boat if we needed it. While we were talking 6 scuba divers stopped close to us and were about to dive in when Phillip one of my pals asked if he could join them and they said sure. Phillip said he would be back with them and we waited right there for Phillip to return ten to fifteen minutes later. As soon as they were in the water their boat upped anchor and disappeared, where did they go. Any way no need to panic. We waited about half an hour for Phillip to surface and swim back to us. Time ticked bye, and no one. Phillip had promised to come back to where we were. I would stand up and look one side of our tender, then sit down and stand up and watch the other side of the tender. As I did this, the swell lifted me up and down, and I could see for a long way around me. Shaun, my remaining pal, and I would take turns to stand up and scan the surface of the water looking for Phillip. There were no signs for any of the other scuba divers either. And by this time, we were panicking. We had lost our buddy to the sea. Shaun and I were there for roughly one and a half hours looking and hoping. Nothing. Then a small speck on the water heading our way was the other scuba divers' dive boat. He came alongside and said he had picked them up a long way away and taken everyone back to shore, and Phillip was fine. Now was the time to get pissed, but very pleased our buddy was safe. Here is his story. "Andy, when I came up for air, we were a long way away from you and when the swell had him (his head alone) at the top of the swell, I was looking the opposite direction, then the next time he was up on a swell I was again looking in the opposite direction." He had to swim a little further away because his air was shorter than all the other guys, but their boat was closer. The captain said he would take all of them in and then come back and tell me, that everyone was fine and back on firm land.

Shaderak:

Shaderak was the name of a local guy we met at Carbo des Quareantes, this is part of Jangamo close to Inhambane. It takes two days to get to Inhambane in Mozambique from Durban by car and we would always go by beach buggy. Coming back fourteen miles from Inhambane, you need to go off road and the road is very soft beach sand a maze of coconut palms and fish eagles, then the road opens onto a beach with a huge natural reef curving out to sea and turning north creating a huge pool of water that cleans every twelve hours at spring high tide. It is twenty feet deep, but the sides are up to twelve feet deep, covered in soft and hard corals and the world's most gorgeous marine fish. This is what we were after, the smaller reef fish for our large tanks at home. This natural reef is called "Carbo des Quareantes," and it is gorgeous. There is a small thatch roofed shelter that four people can squeeze into and we also had our own pup tents to sleep in, if it got wet. We had just settled in when Shaderak arrived and said he would do all our cooking and anything else we wanted him to do for twenty-five cents each day. Mozambique is super poor, and eight years after this, the country went into a revolution, but we did not know a revolution was imminent in 1971. There were coconut trees all around us, so one day around noon I asked Shaderak if he would get us four coconuts. "Yes, sir." Then Shaderak and his dog started to run along this five-mile curved beach. Shaderak and his dog got smaller and smaller until they eventually disappeared. One hour turned into two hours, two turned into three and round 5.00 p.m. in the far distance we could see a small figure and a dog coming our way along the same beach where Shaderak had disappeared. Yes, this was Shaderak and as he got closer, we could see the four coconuts.

As he walked into camp with a huge smile, I asked him a question. "Shaderak, there are coconut trees all around us, and I could have possibly climbed the one closest to us. Why did you not take these coconuts here?" "No sir, those coconuts belong to someone else, if they catch me taking their coconuts, they cut off my hand." These coconuts are from my yard at my home. These were the best tasting coconuts ever. "Thank you Shaderak." We named Shaderak. "Rolling Thunder" after that because he is the speaker of truth.

When this trip was over, we naturally over-paid Shaderak and I gave him one pair of black boxer shorts and one red T-shirt plus other clothes. We returned to Cabo des Quareantes two years later to the same spot, and Shaderak appeared as if we booked him. He stood in khaki shorts and a very faded brown T-shirt. I did notice just a little red on that t-shirt and asked him. "Shaderak is this the same pair of black shorts and red T-shirt I gave you two years ago?" "OH yes, sir, it is. Then he started to tell us a story about his new clothes he got from me two years earlier. "Sir, when you gave me these pants and my nice new red T-shirt, I went home very happy." When he walked into his house (which was possibly a mud hut) his wife and daughter were hiding away on the ground under blankets. They had seen this man far away coming near their house in black pants and a red shirt and did not know this man, so they were very fearful. "Sir, I have worn these pants and this shirt for every day since I saw you the last time. Rolling Thunder had a simple life.

One unfortunate incident I created was to follow and try to catch a lemon spot that was a little on the large side, but I wanted it, so I stuck with trying to catch this smart fish. The out-cropping of rocks had a large section two-thirds the way along, when the tide turned the sea water would be forced through this large opening, bringing in clean water at every high tide. This gap was forty feet wide so lots of water spewed in and out at spring high and low tides. In the morning it was easy to cross and at 1.00 pm it was difficult because you were tired from being in the water for three to four hours. I had spent all three hours trying to catch this gorgeous lemon-spot butterfly fish and eventually I got it. Not smart on my part, but until you put yourself in this position, you do not realize what you have done. It was now totally impossible to swim across that gap without getting dragged out to sea via the beach, so I stood on the rock and waved at my buddies on the beach. One of the girls waved back at me. Kindly know, there is not one sole within twenty miles each way, because no one comes here. I had decided to stand on the last large rock until 23.00 p.m. that night when the tide changed again. I was totally exhausted from diving down ten feet for three hours and trying to catch my lemon spot. So, I stood, and I stood, and just then a speed boat came near the tip. I waved to him to come to me. He did and I shouted asking him to kindly take me to shore, I was far too exhausted to swim to shore, even if it looked close. The push of the incoming tide was pushing this lagoon water out to sea and I was on the tip of the reef. He said, "Okay swim to my boat." I did and climbed in. He said, "You know it is totally impossible that I was going to be here today." His wife was in the boat as well admiring the fish in my transparent catch box and he said, He had heard of this reef and wanted to see it, but his wife did not want to go so far from where they were camped. Luckily for me he begged her to go with him I thanked them very much and jumped off the speedboat and waded to shore. In all the camping trips we every did to Carbo des Quareantes, I never saw another soul on the beach, or in the wooded coconut groves, or any boat pass bye, even ten miles out to sea. Oh yes, someone was looking after me.

Changing from marine fish, 1970-1973 back to motor cycle racing.

Simon Fourie:

In 1972 Gaile and I lived in Halrozby Court, corner Point Road and West Street. One afternoon I had just picked up my 1971 Hudson Hornet from the garage where it was parked. I heard this voice say, "Andy Buys." This strange voice belonged to Simon Fourie, who was not only going to be my best buddy for many years; but also, my adopted son, as Simon needed a good family life. Simon was in a taxi and was putting himself through college by running a taxi. To this day very little is known about Simon's parents' brothers and or sisters. Simon had been coming to the race track and had seen me racing to remember my name. Simon became a judge and was working in Kwa Mashu area doing court cases. One day when Gaile and I had moved into our Sherwood home, Simon arrived with five hundred white T-shirts. Andy we are going to print Skunk Rally on all these T-s hirts, so the week-end was spent printing Skunk Rally T-shirts. Simon and I went to the Skunk Rally, which he had set up for motor cyclists to have fun over a week-end.

Those rallies were not my cup of tea, but I did what I had to do to assist Simon where possible. In 1974 Simon also went motor cycle racing, so we saw each other all over the place, all the time.

Mike Dobbs of TV:

One day Simon Fourie called me from Johannesburg and said he talked to Mike Dobbs (South African Televisions most well-known TV news presenter and broadcaster) you can liken Mike Dobbs to Walter Cronkite, but Mike was young and superbly handsome. Mike Dobbs was coming to Durban, and Simon had sent him directly to my home to stay for the night. Okay, we were far older then Mike, who also brought his girlfriend. I called my wife's best buddy who owned the Langoustine Restaurant in Queensborough, and she said, "Come and have dinner with us, whatever you eat or drink, is on the house." I said thanks and suggested we shoot out for dinner at the langoustine. Mike loved that idea. We were led to our table and a wonderful evening unveiled. As I walked out, I thanked my friend and Dobbs, "the dirt bag," never thanked my friends for the meal. Oh well, he must have felt very entitled. A few days later my friend told me she had invited all her friends to the restaurant to see Mike Dobbs, but not to make it obvious he was around. It dawned on me that no one seemed to know we were there, so a good time was enjoyed by all. Thank you, Simon, for sending Mike Dobbs over to our home. It was good to meet him personally, but he needed some manners.

SPORT: IS THE BACKBONE TO BUSINESS

Motorcycle Racing, 1974 Onwards:

By 1972, I had built my first home using a builder. Gaile and I moved in with both little girls, Debbie and Susan. January 3 of 1974 I felt I would like to start racing a 125-cc racing bike, plus I ordered leathers from England. So early 1974, I was ready to race again, in a small way. I never do thing in a small way. I was soon enjoying racing the smaller bikes, so a 500-cc production Yamaha bike was added to my stable. When compared to another 500-cc bike my brand-new Yamaha was slow. I then purchased a 250 Yamaha racer TD2. I was riding smarter now, but hated the drum-brakes, of that era. Even the factory supplied racing bikes with front wheel drum-brakes. Gosh, I hated them. Drum brakes were good for one lap, then they faded. Added to this frustration was the two strokes of the day, had zero back-wheel slow-down power. Drum-brakes never worked well no matter how large the were. Things changed with Suzuki South Africa (the major dealer in the land) gave me a 250-cc production Suzuki to race for them. I added the new water cooled TZ 250-cc Yamaha racer direct from the factory in Japan. Now both bikes had front and back disc brakes, and that changed the sport. You could rely on disc brakes which meant breaking far later than normal and doing that lap after lap. My first race on this TZ racer I won the race and I won all the 250 production races to be Natal champion on 1977. In 1978 I won the production championship to become the South African champion. Suzuki gave me a 750-cc production bike and I beat everyone in that class for that year 1979. Up to 1980, Suzuki was paying me $550 for each race and supplying the bikes. For 1980 Suzuki offered me their new I,100-cc production bike. No money was offered and my overall-plans had changed. I was looking to build a super-large home to make money. Had Suzuki offered me money, as well as the bike, I would have raced another year, or two. In 1979, I was also thirty-eight years old and at my peak performance. In my last two years of racing, I never fell off once, but had got used to riding on the limit all the time. In those years of racing, I did have one crash, where another gentleman took out my front wheel and I hit the tar with my right shoulder, breaking my other collar-bone, and concussing me again, but this time racing was almost slate-free of crashes.

The easiest racing motorcycle to race was a 7-R 350 machine. It was easy on the front brakes because of the large back-wheel stopping power, when gearing down. Unfortunately, the Japanese motor-cycles of the day were two strokes, and they were a lot faster than those older motorcycles, also with zero back-wheel stopping from the engine.

Racing Boredom and Fun:

Traveling to Rhodesia, now known as Zimbabwe, we raced there twice and what lovely people and lovely race tracks. We were off to Salisbury and their major race-track just outside that town. While traveling, if you saw a friend in front of you hauling his two motor cycles behind their car on an open trailer, everyone in our car (normally three of us) would search for ammunition. Ammunition was baked beans, tomatoes, raw eggs, and just anything we can throw at them as we pass. Okay everyone had something in their hands. I overtook our pals also on their way to Rhodesia (Zimbabwe). As we got past them, we all stretched out our windows and threw baked beans, raw eggs, soft tomatoes, and anything that could make a mess, of the car. Once we were passed, we traveled for ten maybe fifteen minutes well ahead of them, looking back to make sure they could see us. We then looked for a good fly-over pass-way. This had to be done correctly, or you get seen. We are far up front of our pals, so they did not know what we were planning. We pulled off the highway and waited for them to go past, and once they had gone in front of us, we pulled back onto the highway and loaded up with more ammunition for attack number two.

Generally, they did not know we were back behind them until you over-took them again. This second time was also a surprise, we threw our beans and tomatoes at them for a second time. Ha-ha. When stopping later in the day to refuel, they pulled in behind us and the gasoline attendants would not serve them gasoline. "Why did you not serve gasoline to our friends?" I asked. "Sir, someone had puked all over their car, it was too dirty." We cracked up laughing, knowing our buddies had to refill their own car with gasoline and also to clean their windows. At all service stations, there were gasoline attendants who filled up your gas tank, cleaned your windscreen and also checked your oil and water.

During practice in Salisbury, Zimbabwe, I noticed a bird sitting in the middle of this 120-mile-an-hour sweep. A sweep is a long curve where your knee is on the tar and your head and part of your body are on the right-hand side of the bike. Not to hit, the bird you had to lift your knee at the apex of this fast corner. Every single time all the bikes went past, the bird was there tweeting at each one of us. I knew it was a mother protecting her young, so after practice, I walked back to the spot found momma bird now running to me and on the ground were two fluffy baby chicks huddled to the ground. I shooed them further away from the race track, and the next day during the actual race, mommy bird was not there, she was further away from the race track. Then in Cape Town at Killarney race track (not to be confused by Kyalami). Kyalami means my home and is in Johannesburg, many miles away from Cape Town. I noticed a dik-kop standing close to the circuit, and she was in the same place all the time. A dik-kop is a nocturnal bird and the name means thick head. They are seen during the day but fleetingly. I also walked to where Mrs. Dik-kop was standing close to her nest, there were two small chicks, which must have just hatched a few days earlier.

Raw Howard:

All the motorcycle racers' wives, used to sit high on the bleachers, or grand stands at a corner where their men were traveling at 120 miles per hour. This incident was at Kayalami race circuit in Johannesburg, and these grand stands were at Sunset bend. Their steel frame work held up wooden seating for crowds of people. Raw Howard was sitting on the top wooden seat with her hands between her two upper legs, all by herself and just away from other people during one of the noon practice sessions, and I was on my way to sit next to her. She had no idea I was coming, so I climbed up under the seating with my hands holding on to the three-inch steel supports. There was a very big problem with this. That did not alarm me up, until I had to go down, but that later. As I was pulling myself up, I had to stretch up and behind me, and every time I let go of the lower beam support, my body weight would swing away from the last beam. Gravity was doing its work on the way up. Very difficult but I got to the top just under Raw (her real given name) Under Raw's body, now I was so close I could see both her hands clasping both the inside of each upper leg. To give her a fright, I grabbed both her inner legs just inside of where she was holding her own legs. You have never heard a louder scream, Whhhhaaa. And I was breaking down laughing, also trying to go down, but now I was laughing and trying to grasp the lower beam, which was away from my body and also far lower down. How I never fell three or four times, I will never know but I did get down and ran away, shouting, "I did it, I did it!" still laughing. I knew I nearly broke many bones right there or could have killed myself had I let go or slipped.

I also knew that one day Raw and I would have a good laugh about that shock she got. We did many years later. She lived with her husband, Ofie Howard in Rhodesia/Zimbabwe, so she came to many races.

Peter Ekerold and I went away together three times over our racing years, Peter also had a TD2 racing bike from the Yamaha factory. Everyone is Peters friend, so he and I had a good few miles together. On one occasion I picked up Peter at his home, my bike was already on the trailer behind my orange hornet GMC 1971 car. Peter loaded his bike with my assistance, and it was firmly tied down. We were off ready to race in Johannesburg at Kayalami race circuit, in Johannesburg. We had not been traveling for too long when we went down a long hill fifteen miles from his home, and we were obviously over the speed limit. Out stepped a policeman and waved us to stop. I slowed down and stopped just past him. He came over to the driver's side window and said, "License and insurance sir." I gave him what he asked for and before looking at my driver's license he said, "Speeding sir?" "Yes officer." He looked at my driver's license and said, "Are you Spencer Buys son?" "Yes, sir I am." "Andrew?" "Yes," and I looked carefully at the man, "It is me Hector Pollard, I used to come to your home and have lunch when I was in the Army and your dad was my sergeant major." I did recognize Hector and he was a great guy from many years back. "Okay I will let you off your ticket, but go slower, and give my regards to your mom and dad." "Okee-dokee," and off Peter and I went. This incident has always remained with Peter and me.

Peter Ekerold:

Peter loved being a salesman ay Charlie Young Yamaha. I had first met Charlie Young when he was selling Suzuki motorcycles at Jones tire company building around 1962 or 1963 and he moved his company a few years later to the corner of Smith Street. It was here that Peter practiced his trade of selling motorcycles. Here is how Peter explained to me what transpired at work one day. "Geez Andy, I felt so bad today. I sold a soft-spoke, very nice African gentleman a 125-cc motorcycle. I did the paper work and asked him how he was going to pay. He pulled out a sack full of coins, pennies, quarters, fifty-cent pieces, and a few notes and said he had been saving up for many years to purchase his motor- cycle. It took them forever to count the money and it was correct." Peter asked the soft-spoken gentleman if he could ride a motorcycle, his reply was. "Yes." So, Peter inserted the keys and started the motor, which had a full fuel tank of gas. The motorcycle was quietly ticking over, and the gentleman mounted the machine inside the showroom and opened the throttle, then dropped the clutch. Both the motorcycle and the soft-spoken gentleman flew through the entire showroom floor window. The motorcycle lay screaming outside the shop until Peter stepped through the broken window to switch off the machine. Peter was shocked at what had just transpired and was trembling, he hunched over to pull the gentleman up off the pavement. "Sir, you said you could ride a motor- cycle." "Yes, sir, I was too shy to tell you I just got my license, but I forgot what to do." The motorcycle did not have too many new scratches, so Peter took him around the block and the man eventually rode his new motorcycle home.

The Pool and the Excited Motorcyclist:

Our city had Yamaha motorcycles that ended up as delivery bikes and they were normally the smaller 125-cc motorcycles easy on fuel and very reliable. I was talking to a pool company secretary in the building right next to Charlie Young motor-cycles, and this pool company had set up a cement pool within their show-room that was level with the floor. It was a magnificent example of their craft and their pool had a small rockery at one end and steps into the pool at the other. The entrance was a glass door and a huge shop front window next to the entrance door, so when walking past you could see the pool and the lady behind the desk across the pool brightly lit up. Very well done. One day an African delivery gentleman had to deliver a small package to this pool company, and I happened to be at the secretary's desk. The front door opened with a bang and a gentleman ran towards us with outstretched parcel in his hand. He did not see the swimming pool in front of him and ran directly onto the swimming pool clothes, package and all. Water was splashed all over the place and up came an African gentleman puzzled as can be, dripping water all-over the place. "I am so sorry madam, I did not see the pool!" We just cracked up laughing and he was so apologetic, we said, "Not to worry." Years later that pool company changed into a Kawasaki dealership.

Robert Baker:

We had traveled to the Aldo Scribante race track in Port Elizabeth and we raced there every year. At a guess the year was 1979, and we were at the normal Friday practice. Once practice was over on the afternoon, the track was open for everyone. Anthony Fourie and myself had taken my truck to the outside of the fastest sweep at the Aldo Scribante race circuit to watch other guys do a few laps. Anthony and I were very impressed with Rob Baker he was flying through this flat-out 100 mile-an-hour sweep and in the past, he found it very hard to learn the narrow power band of the racing Yamaha motorcycle. We agreed that today Rob had made the grade as he looked really looked good. It was the very first stages of getting dark, plus we had a lot to do before heading back to our hotel for the night. We got into my truck and followed the road to the tunnel under the race track, as we went through, I notice Rob Baker against the bank of the tunnel. It was clear Rob had made a mistake through that fast sweep and had held onto his bike even when he was off the circuit and hit the protection barrier wall and he had gone over the wall in the air and landed twenty feet below against the bank. This must have just happened, and he was already blue in the face with purple lips. I said to Anthony, "You wait here, do what you can, and I will go and look for a doctor." I shot off to the pits and ran around shouting for a doctor. I found one and said, "Please come with me. A man has had a bad accident," and he jumped into the passenger seat. While going back to Rob Baker, the doctor told me it was almost impossible that he was at the race track that day, he was not supposed to be there. It was also late, so all medical staff had left sometime back. The doctor had asked his pal to follow us with his own car. Rob Baker died that day. So good friend rest in peace your pals have never forgotten you.

The Bee Swarms:

Motor-cycle racing in Port Elizabeth at the Aldo Scribante race circuit, I was in a race and went through a large swarm of bees. Traveling at 130 Miles-per-hour you have no warning and immediately hit this swarm of bees. Some splat on your visor and you can feel them hit your arms shoulders and the motorcycles screen is also splattered with a good few of them. You cannot stop and simply keep on going, then one stings you on the neck, and another has somehow found its way up your arm and also stings you, then a second sting on your opposite shoulder, and you have to wait for the final six laps to be complete before you can pull out the sting. On both occasions my mechanics were waiting for me as I got off the track, so I jumped off the bike and took off my helmet to attend to the bee on my neck first. Peter Herman, one of my best pals, took hold of my bike, and I shouted a word which flipped out my front teeth. The teeth clopped on the tar, and I quickly picked them up and flopped them back in my mouth, before too many people saw what transpired. Peter cracked up laughing. Teeth went back in my mouth, then had time to attend to the bee stings. There were so many bees, I cannot work out how they could get up my arm or under my leathers to sting my neck and shoulder. This also happened in Johannesburg when racing at Kyalami, we were in Africa after all.

Practicing at the Race-track on a Week-day.

The race track was open during the week and anyone could go and do laps at the circuit and at Roy Hesketh circuit (named after a war hero Roy Hesketh who was awarded the Victoria Cross). At the same place on different days I had two different mishaps. The first was the longest green mamba crossing the Pietermaritzburg straight, and I aimed at the snake, which was almost the length width of the race- track. I wondered if I ran over the snake, could it strike and bury its deadly fangs into me? I did not take that chance I made sure I missed the snake. The snake ran to the infield of the circuit. On a second occasion, a gorgeous big brown ridge-back dog waggling it' tail happily. Oh no, dog, I am going one hundred miles per hour here, and then he ran totally across my path and was exactly sideways to me. I hit the dog side-on and went totally over the dog with both wheels. I rode back to the pits and got my mechanic to come with me to see how the dog was. The dog was alive and showing no pain, but it was clear his back was broken so we took him to a vet in Pietermaritzburg. I explained what had transpired so that the vet knew how the dog was hurt. The dog had a collar with telephone number, and we left the dog with the vet. I knew the dog would be put down.

SPORT: IS THE BACKBONE TO BUSINESS

The Factory Works Honda and Jim Redman:

One day (Gentleman Jim, was his nickname) Jim Redman, M.B.E. (six times world champion on a Honda four), was at the track practicing. Paddy Driver was there, and a longtime friend of Jim Redman's, and so was my sister Diane and her husband, Tommy Johns. Jim went around the circuit a few laps and came in and gave the bike to Tommy John's to ride. Marlen Redman and my sister were sitting talking on the wall and Jim said to Paddy Driver. "Take her for a few laps, when Tommy is finished." Paddy did the world race tracks with Jim Redman in 1961 to 1963 and came third to Mike Hailwood in those days, so they were good friends for many years. "Andy, when Paddy gets back, you can also take a few laps on my factory Honda 4." Tommy did his laps, and Paddy did a few laps and came in to say the bike had seized as he was coming through the sweep, so by a hair I missed riding one of the world's top factory race bikes. The famous factory works Honda 4 Given to Jim Redman a few years earlier.

Welcome Race Way:

The gold mines in the town of Welcome, wanted all sports available to all their staff and so it was. They built this gorgeous Welcome race-track. Traveling at night was done every Thursday night so that we got to the race track to practice at 9.00 a.m. on a Friday. At two o-clock one dark morning I saw an owl sitting in the middle of the road. I did a U-turn with the race bikes on the trailer. I went back to where I had seen the owl and did a second U-turn and now faced the owl a second time. I got out the vehicle and walked behind the owl, so the owl was facing the car lights. I picked her up and knew she had a broken wing.

The Welcome Race Way is in the middle of nowhere. So, we had to do all practice on a Friday and on the Saturday, we race at the official meeting go to prize giving and either travel home immediately afterward, or the next day which is a Sunday. I would have to study the birds broken wing late on Sunday. Well we had plenty of owl food for the owl. When the Formula 1 race cars and their large motor homes went through the tunnel and under the race track tunnel to get to the pits, their large motor homes would rip down a good few swallow mud nests and the dead babies were on the ground. I collected a few baby swallows and put them on ice. We left the owl in the vehicle during practice. The owl had not moved in one and a half hours. She was just sitting there, so I force fed the owl as she did not want to eat. She did eat.

Barry Coleman wanted to go into a small 7-Eleven shop a few miles up the road, so I said sure take the truck, if Barry Kerr held the owl on his lap. That was the deal. When they got back, Barry Kerr gave me hell, "Andy, I do not want to touch that bird again." "Why Barry?" "Well it did a number two all over my lap and have you any idea what that smells like?" "I do as I had owned a barn owl, and this was a wood owl. Their number two was a wet white guano that got squirted all over the place and it smells like heck. We cracked up laughing, but Barry Kerr was not a happy chappie. The owl passed away on race day, and I was then able to examine the wound. This wood owl was hit by a car or truck and her wing broke. When the wing broke, the open bone went into her lungs as her body was badly pierced by the wing bone, which meant she had internal bleeding. The poor bird was a mess, but we did not know this before we could have a careful look.

John Baker, My Famous Mechanic and Dear Friend Forever;

The best family we ever went to stay with were the McInnes family. John McInnes also started racing round the same time as me. So, we used to end up in the same positions at various racetracks around South Africa. John had a sister named Carol and John's Mom was the fire in this family who held the entire family together. Antoinette was her name who we all loved. She was also the perfect host, she loved having John Baker and I there to sleep, over race-week-ends. We were clean living and she knew we were a good influence on her son and family. We would be fed the best breakfast then all of us would go to practice. John's dad was also John, and he was always there assisting his son John. Early to bed after practice on the Friday, all looking forward to the race on the following day. John's dad was the quiet gentleman who loved watching the competition and he was keen to see John do better and better. John's dad was a builder of homes in their town of Bloemfontein (a town in the state of Transvaal). Every morning would be a huge spread of beacon and, various egg dishes, so a hearty breakfast was ready for everyone to select from. One morning John Baker, my mechanic, got hold of me before breakfast and said to me, "Andy, no matter what you do at breakfast, do not say one word." "Why?" "Well, remember that little girl of 16 that was here last night?" "Yeah."

"Well we stayed here long after everyone had gone to bed, and she and I got caught with her bar down and may hands on her breasts. Mrs. Antoinette McInnes switched on the lights and caught us." "She was not happy and sent the little girl home. I put my tail between my legs and feel so bad I was caught especially by her. Please do not say one word." I never mentioned it. That morning breakfast was exactly as it normally was. Antoinette passed away the following year in her sleep and she was young, charming, polite, and beautiful. We were all shocked, we never went to John's McInnes's home again. The following year, John McInnes junior, my dear friend, was killed by a driver shooting a green light, and his dad went to pieces. I did see Carol one year into her marriage about four years later and she said her dad was not treating her well. I explained the poor man lost the will to live. He lost his lover, and his son, and his will to go on was no longer there for the man. This was a family vanishing, like shadows before the rain. Here is a tragedy, because this entire family and the drive to live was gone and this lovely family just disintegrated. Mr. John McInnes Sr. had drifted away from his daughter, Carol, so this entire family was gone forever. I never saw Carol again, but I am sure; she has two wonderful children and a man who loves her. It is not likely our paths will ever cross again, but I do hope they do. When I was seventy years old, I stayed one evening with John Baker and his charming wife and family. John certainly selected the nicest girl in the neighborhood to marry. When we had a quiet moment together, I asked John Baker about that night Antoinette caught him with the little girl, and he admitted he was caught being naughty with that little girl. It was far worse than John first told me. I am so pleased I did not know then. I would have felt a lot worse than I did, so thank you, John.

Mike Grant, Mike the Bike:

Mike the Bike earned that nick name as he did some wonderful motor cycle racing, making world champions feel a little inferior. I mention this because at one race meeting, Giacomo Agostini, the major world champion, was racing his famous MV Augusta at our home circuit. Mike rode around the man at the Beacon Bend and lead the man through the sweep onto the main straight of our home circuit and Mike told me, that Ago opened the throttle and left him far behind. The MV Augusta, was so fast. I saw Mike do that a few times and he was some motorcycle racer. I say was because he still is, but he is also seventy-three or four years old now. Mike married three times and I attended every wedding he had. He invited me to his second bulls party before his 2 (second) wedding to Maggie Grant. We all remain dear friends today even after divorces and new marriages. Anyway, Mike said his bulls' party was at the prestige men's club in Durban called the Men's Club, which was in the middle of the city of Durban and very high-end. Mike said to me, "Andy, you have to wear jacket, tie and long trousers to get into the club." "There are guards on the door, and they do not let you in without long trousers, tie and a jacket, so you really have to look the part." "Okay Mike, will do." I wanted a way around this, and I did have a three-quarter long thick Double-faced wool duffel coat, with wooden toggles to close off the front.

This was perfect for what I had in mind. I put on a perfect white lounge shirt. Then cut the shirt all the way around at a man's nipple level. I put on a soft-colored blue tie and cut off the tie at the same level as the shirt. This means when you close the double-faced duffel coat you would see a high-end lounge shirt as well as a tie and this would be easily acceptable to get into the Gentlemen's club. This is back in 1977 so there are no girls at this gentlemen's club. Now for the long trouser pants. First, I put on one of those tiny swimming trunks, I drew on a set of long pants and then cut off the legs at the knees. I then removed the long trouser pants and sewed white bandages from my skimpy under-pants to the end of the long pants ends. And I had to do that four times to each leg so that the long plants legs stayed in place and did not swing, or twist around. Now when my double-faced wool duffel coat was buttoned closed with the wooden toggles, I looked the part, nicely dressed, with lounge shirt, blue tie, coat and long pants. I knew I would get into the fancy men's club (men only). If I opened the double-faced coat, then I would be naked almost naked, from my chest all the way down to my knees, except for the smallest set of swimwear under-pants and two white, strings holding up each long pants leg. You could not see the two white bandages at the back holding up the two trouser legs. There were four to each leg. Socks and shoes finished this outfit.

I walked in just a professional as can be and right past the two guards at the door. Once inside, I opened my coat for Mike the Bike, and he broke down. "Hey, Mike you wanted tie and coat, how's this, pal?" Mike had me stand on the table and flash the parents. I knew his dad well, but had never met Maggie's dad, but all the men at this table just packed up laughing. I had to flash a few times during the evening, and as I walked out past the guards, I gave them a naked look as well. Not happy.

All the racing stories happened between 1974 and the end of 1979.

The wild man of our era:

Jon Ekerold had three brothers and a sister, Peter, David and Guido, the eldest and Karen, one of the strongest characters of a woman I have ever met, and she had to be with four wild brothers. All did motor cycle racing and Jon Ekerold went on to be the first, and only man in the world, not supported by a factory, in the 350 class to win the world championship in 1980. Peter raced motorcycles, David Raced motorcycles and Karen married Alan North, also a man who did the world 350 championship in the same year and won one Grad Prix. Alan led, both the 250 and 350 class of the world championship in 1978. So Alan was also the man in those same years. Guido was the only brother not to do the sport. I worked out many years later why one man strives to be a world champion and others do not. When I raced motor cycles it was for fun and I wanted my pals to know I was good at what I did. Racing at the various Moto GP world circuits did not enter my mind, but Jon had a very strong desire to be the best in the world. It is all in the individuals mind. Mentioning Jon Ekerold is not about Motorcycles, it is about the man, that is why this background is needed. Jon loved his whiskey, so he over did things now and again. The Ekerold family lived in Kloof some fifteen miles outside of Durban, the city center. All the nightlife was in the city center. One-night Jon stepped over the line with his Whiskey, and at midnight he decided to go back into the city center, but his car was a wreck, so he snuck into his dads' garage and took his dad's favorite Mercedes and headed back into Durban. It was 1 a.m. now. The highway ended at the outskirts of the city at a large four way-light. At this light the four-way highway went into three smaller lanes into town and the light was set on a short sturdy pole on an island, immediately in front of Jon, on the opposite side of the highway, where there were only three lanes. Jon had stopped his dad's Mercedes on the last fast lane of the highway. When the light changed, he was supposed to glide across into the smaller road way, but he floored the gas pedal and screamed across the intersection taking out the light pole and totaling his dad's favorite Mercedes. The middle of the car had hit the light pole dead center. The police were on the scene and took the drunk man to jail. At 3.00 a.m. Jon called his dad and said, "Dad I am in jail, will you come and pick me up?" "Yes, Jon, I will be there in a jiffy." "Dad, dad, I also took your car." "What?" "Sorry dad, my car keys are on the dresser, your car is a wreck." No need to say one more word about this situation. The reason for telling this story was not to hurt Jon or his family in anyway, but to share what two naughty boys did in their live. Every year Jon made the effort to pop in and see me at the end of his racing season and share a few good tales with me. Jon Ekerold was given Springbok colors in 1978 at a dinner in Johannesburg, and I was awarded the South African Production Champion ship at that same dinner.

The Car and Driveway - 1976:

In 1972 when we moved into our new 51 Loon Road home in Sherwood Durban, our driveway was so steep, I had to call it a pathway to get the plans approved, and this happened after the house was totally complete. They would not let me move in until I had a completion certificate. The drive had a large curve, and it was super steep that many of my friends would not drive up the drive but rather park in the road below and walk up sixty feet to get to the house. I had perched the house as high as possible for the view, and the hard tar driveway was first to be done. This was possibly the steepest drive-way in all of Durban plus that large curve. Gaile had an old Anglia, the same as my 1964 Anglia but yellow with white top. One morning I was running late for work and my normal car was having a service, so I jumped into Gaile's yellow Anglia to go to work in town. As I started to go down our historic notorious driveway, the brake pedal went straight for the floor, so I knew the brakes had failed. The car was already starting to gather speed before the big turn to the left, and I knew that lead to larger issues. I turned hard left to hit the huge bank on my left. The car did not hit the bank like I thought it would. It lifted the left front wheel slowly up the bank and as the wheel climbed higher, it continued to slow. Then the right front wheel tucked under and the car rolled over onto the roof. Seats, lipstick, sunglasses from the glove box, change, and a few ball point pens flopped down onto me, because I was on the ceiling, with my feet in the air. The car was sliding down the tar driveway screaming metal on tar all the way around the curve and to the very bottom of the driveway. The car ended up all four wheels pointing to the heavens next to the mail box, and I managed to climb out one window, walk back up the driveway open the garage, and take my blue scrambler motorcycle to Charlie Youngs Motorcycle dealership, where most of my friends were. I explained what had transpired and asked all the staff to come to my home at 5.30 p.m. that day to turn Gaile's car onto its wheels. Every staff member was at my home laughing seeing a car's feet pointing to the heavens at the foot of my own driveway. All of us just turned it up-right again. Now the vehicle had a flat roof with millions of scraps on the roof, we bumped the huge roof dent out with our hands, but the scares remained. I got into the driver's seat and turned the key, and the car purred into life.

I notice mail in the mail box. Imagine the mailman; turning the corner and seeing a car on her roof, wheels pointed skywards, not a good sight. No one was around. It was as if the vehicle was simply parked there; but upside down. One more mailman story for that mailman.

In 1978 I purchased a piece of ground in Umhlanga Rocks and started to build foundations with my own contractors. I decided to hand the entire home to be built by the Benz Brothers, whom I was drawing plans for, and this home was being completed in late 1979. I had just been to see a fellow draftsman Brian Stadler, and Brian had just completed a huge home, which I could just see big dollar signs. No matter what you paid for a new home and new ground, when done correctly, they will always double; or treble your money. Now I had the money bug. I knew we were going to move into the house we were building in Umhlanga Rocks, and I also wanted to build an even larger home. The plan was to emerge with a bunch of money.

At the end of 1979 when Suzuki offered me their new 1,100 Suzuki and no money was mentioned, I said, no thanks. Now I could concentrate on my large money home in Lower La Lucia. I had paid the, La Lucia, land off in full, with the saved $40,000 and now we had a new home for 1980 in Umhlanga as well. In 1983 we sold our new home for $100,000 more than what we paid for it. So now we looked to build 20 Ridge Road Lower La Lucia. I soon learned it was more profitable building new homes, with the daily business being the cash flow to support what I was doing. We rented a home for a few months and moved into Ridge Road in 1983 and sold in 1999, making $300,000 in that process and lived rent-free, plus I had three other homes under construction.

SPORT: IS THE BACKBONE TO BUSINESS

Durban to Johannesburg:

Simon Fourie wanted to do the fastest time from the center of Durban to the center of Johannesburg, so he asked me to also attend the start of his first attempt, and naturally he stayed at my home the night prior, so all of us could wake up in time to get going.

At the start, he had arranged for Pastor Rene Changuion and me to be at the start of this attempt. At exactly 5.00 a.m. Simon hit the throttle wide open, and his 1,100-cc Suzuki motorcycle roared into life. At this early morning hour, there were zero cars on the road and the city was asleep. The clock watch was set, and Simon was looking at traveling 614 kilometers through cities on major roads at 290 kilometer per hour and filling up his motorcycle with gasoline at various planned stops. Simon had taped twenty cent pieces to his handlebars to throw into the toll booths, and he had more than enough coins for that. At the very last-minute, Simon had me tape one gallon of gasoline to his side, because the fuel was worrying him. Now Simon was also a ticking time bomb. He was determined to make Johannesburg under three hours. This is much faster than the cannon ball run in the Bandits Trans-Am.

The screaming of his motorcycle could be heard for the first fifteen miles, so I was surprised no police caught the man. Simon's wife was very unhappy with this plan. His motor cycle blew up the first time he attempted to get this done and the second time the gearbox started to slip close to home, but his third attempt, he made it. Simon Fourie will always be the only man to do Durban to Johannesburg in two hours and fifty-nine minutes and ten seconds. The times were synchronized by Pastor Rene Changuion and his counter-part in Johannesburg. I was at each start of these Durban to Johannesburg illegal runs. Two hours fifty-nine minutes and ten seconds, center to center. Under three hours, this record is likely never to be beaten. Simon Fourie has his own Radio program. He is the editor of South Africa's top motor cycling magazine, possibly the top magazine in South Africa. Simon Fourie has been my number one pal since we first met in 1970. He would arrive at my home and start to make flap-Jacks (pan cakes for all), or he would just arrive with two cartons of ice-cream, devour one himself and the other was for us normal people. Simon arrived at our home on a Saturday and said, "Today, we are going to print five-hundred Skunk rally T-shirts!" so off we start to print. T-shirts were hanging everywhere, they were printed and had to dry individually, so hanging space became an issue. This started Simon's Rally career, Simon just did everything to make money and he was smart with his decisions. When Gaile and I left South Africa in 1990, Simon sent us his magazine (BIKE S.A.) every month, no matter where we were in the world, even today (2018), with his final magazine he never missed sending us his magazine. He never asked for one cent in payment, it was just the size of the man's heart. What a man.

Fleas:

During my architectural days, I was associated with The Payne family. David Payne went to school with my sisters and David eventually became one of the top jockeys in South Africa, later to become a trainer and owner of many racehorses. David's Dad, was a builder who had me draw all his plans for many different projects he was doing at the time. One day Mr. Payne drove me to one of the vacant houses he owned in his building truck. This house was in the middle of busy Durban and had been vacant for some time. While inside, Mr. Payne told me what he wanted to do, and I took all measurements, then it was back in the vehicle. We were now on our way home as both of us lived in La Lucia. The time was rush hour at 4.30 p.m., so all the cars were in the road and pavements were full of people. I felt a real funny strange, an abnormal feeling moving up my legs, on the inside of both legs. It was like having goose bumps, but it was different, like each hair on my legs were starting to move up from my calf to my knees. Something was very wrong here. This was a light feeling, and nothing I had ever felt in my life before. Every human being would have also known something was wacky here, this was totally wrong. I looked at the outside of both my trouser legs and I saw fleas, so thick they were on top of each other in a mass and close to my knees on the outside of my longs as well. "Stop the car. Stop the car, quickly now." Mr. Payne had to double-park. I opened the passenger door and dived out of the car ripped off my long trousers.' Keep in mind I had a tie, a lounge shirt, and long trousers on. My jacket was in the back seat of the vehicle. Now I was on the pavement with no long trousers, jumping up and down rubbing a mass of fleas off both legs, first the calves and then each chin, jumping, jumping away from a pair of long trousers lying on the cold concrete pavement. One foot high in the air, the other on the concrete pavement, then the next foot high in the air, shooing off tiny little fleas, off both my legs. When I settled down free of fleas, I looked at a perplexed crowd and looked at Mr. Payne. I have never seen a man laughing so much. He was pounding the steering wheel, possibly wetting his pants. The only one not laughing was me. The huge crowd were not laughing, they had no idea what was going on. I picked up the one corner of my long trousers, using two tips of my fingers, and threw them into the bed of the builder's truck and got back into the passenger's seat naked apart from under- pants. Mr. Payne was still laughing uncontrolled. I now started to laugh at the entire situation. I will never know what the pedestrians thought about this situation which unfolded right in front of them. Only one, or two were laughing, the rest were straight faced.

Once Mr. Payne had settled down, he explained what had just transpired, "Andy, when a home has had dogs and cats then the house is left vacant for as long as that house was; the fleas multiply and all are hungry waiting for dogs and cats to walk by. Both of us were in the house, and I did not get fleas on me, yet you got these masses climb on you. It is clear when you measured the rooms, you entered one heavily infested room that was blowing over with fleas. Well you certainly gave me a good hearty laugh and one I will never forget."

The Lady on the Porch:

I got called out to do an alteration for a lady and the time was 5.00 p.m. so off I went to 24 Meadows Lane. I found 22 Meadows Lane, nice dirt driveway to the house, and no driveway to the next house, and I found 26 Meadows Lane, also with a dirt driveway. The house in the middle must be 24 Meadows Lane, I drove past it again and again and knew there was no road to this house. I could see a lady on the porch. I parked opposite what I felt was 24 Meadows Lane. When I got out of my car there was a ditch with water and bull-rushes on the opposite side of the puddle of water. I had no idea how deep this puddle was, so I walked on through the puddle, and then it was up towards the high green bull- rushes. The puddle was deeper than anticipated. My shoes were totally wet and again my attire was shoes, long trousers, a lounge shirt, a tie, and my jacket was in the car. Okay, so now my shoes were wet, and my long trousers are wet halfway up my calves, but I was at the tall green bull rushes and almost out of the water, that I could see. The bull-rushes were thick, so I pushed my way through and tried to get out of the water and tall green bull rushes. I feel four sharp claws hook onto my inner thigh. The two top hooks are very close to my crutch and the two lower hooks into my skin are just above my knee. These hooks were not deep hooks, but I know something is hanging under my long trouser leg onto my skin. We lived in Darkest Africa, so anything is possible and creepy. I grabbed this thing with one hand as firmly as could be, it was either him or me. I held my trouser leg from the outside as hard as I could and whipped-off my long trousers. The lady on the porch had been watching me walk through the bog and as I stepped out, those long green bull-rushes, off went my pants. It was time to fight the monster inside my long trousers, with both hands. Now I had a chance to look at this animal. I turned the trousers inside out and let go. The biggest praying mantis I have ever seen; it had walked up the inside of my trouser leg, when I walked through the green bull rushes and as I got out to start walking up the slight hill, towards the porch, this praying mantis must have turned around and hooked into my flesh. I had crushed it. The lady on the porch was so perplexed until I told her a praying mantis had climbed up my leg. She said, "Why did you not come up our driveway?" "I could not find your drive way." "Oh, we use the next-door neighbor's drive way." Pity she did not tell me when she called me.

During these days we lived in Sherwood. Sherwood was a great home. We stayed there until I purchased another piece of land in Umhlanga Rocks in Oyster Crescent. I started to build a home there as well and the date was 1979. This date clashed with racing motorcycles; I was using spare cash money to build the new home in Umhlanga, and with the money I made from selling my Sherwood home, I bought land in South Africa's most expensive area, Lower La Lucia and I paid that off in cash and left it to hibernate. Peppermint Palace was five doors north of us. I let this lower La Lucia land lie dormant for three years. In 1980 we were building, and completed, Oyster Crescent and had stopped racing to save money and to slot into building a new home. I certainly could have raced on, but with no money offered by Suzuki I walked away at the end of 1979.

The end of 1979 was basically the end of my sportsman's career. We entered phase two, which was after being a sportsman, phase two was building new homes. The end of phase two developed into murders and rapes, being common place.

A Grand New Home 20 Ridge Road, Lower La Lucia, South Africa, 1984-1999

I walked away from racing, and it was just at the right time. The house I built in 1980 I made a clear $100,000 by 1983, plus I had in the past bought a piece of land in Ridge Road, Lower La Lucia and left it to hibernate. Now was the time to build a super home with a gorgeous view, just off the beach. The new Lower La Lucia home was also the birth-place of my purchase of my Trans-Am Indianapolis Pace car and the black-and-gold Bandit Trans-Am purchased for Gaile, my wife. Gaile did not want this Bandit Trans-Am; that is not who she is; she does not like flash, but I wanted it for her anyway. One day Gaile took Debbie and Susan to drop at school, and as Gaile stopped at the school, three of the mothers who had never spoken with Gaile in the past ran up to her to say. "Wow, Gaile this is a gorgeous car." How shallow people can be. The land at 20 Ridge Road was built on was exceptionally steep, so I built a flat concrete slab, from boundary to boundary, which was flush to the road and going seventy feet out, standing on thirty-three feet high pillars. That was the floor to the grounds and the entire house. The swimming pool was also built on stilts, so was the two-car garage, plus all the yard space for the entire home. The tops of the trees below were thirty-three feet high as well. The gray vervet monkeys used to hop along the tree tops and onto our veranda and steal the fruit from our fruit bowl. Their favorite steal was the sugar bowl, and we often had to watch a monkey until the sugar was finished, to see where the monkey left the empty sugar bowl. In 1984-1989 we lived like kings and queens, the business had taken off, and I sold the both Trans-Am's for double the money paid for them and purchased the top five hundred SEC Mercedes Benz. I had the car for one year, when a major decision was made at the end of 1989 to leave South Africa.

An Unusual Dinner in 1988

Four-times world motor cycling champion Kork Ballington and his wife to day live in Australia. In 1988 Kork and I, plus two other gentlemen did not work on a Friday, so the four of us played tennis. One Saturday evening, I asked Kork and Bronwyn to dinner with us, plus a gentleman (let's call him Dick) Dick and his charming wife, Joan, to enjoy dinner with us. On the Saturday morning, I would collect oysters and the odd lobster from the beach below us. To add to this, we would purchase some huge eight-inch prawns and have a sea food evening. Gaile would cook half the oysters and half would be raw in their shell. A real great evening was held this way, and on this evening, I suggested we tell everyone about the most embarrassing thing that ever happened to us. Immediately Dick said to Joan, "No you cannot tell that one." We pushed him and Joan to tell us what was embarrassing, "No." was their answer. We told our stories of embarrassment. Then we pushed Dick and Joan to tell us their embarrassing story, they did not wish to share with us. The answer was still, "No," from Dick. Joan said, "Okay, let me tell you guys. Dick and I were married at the time, to other partners, and we fell in love with each other.

Well one weekday during lunchtime, Dick and I went looking for a spot to make love. We drove into this quiet park and stopped under a tree for shade, and both of us hopped into the back of the car. We were doing what birds and bees do, and after a little time I had this uneasy feeling and looked out the car side window. To my horror, there were faces pushed up against three windows of the car watching us. *And I was on top.* What had transpired was a college class had come down to the park to do some nature class, and one of the boys had spotted us and the rest followed." Most embarrassing. Kork had introduced Dick to us who happened to live up the road from us. Kork had a red Porsche and Dick was the manager of the local Porsche dealership. After this fun dinner, Dick was caught invoicing a Porche door to be panel beaten and painted, then he pocketed the funds. Dick went to Jail and we never saw them again.

Murder at Our Doorstep

Here is an example; Andre Takis is a dear friend of ours. Andre and his wife had two twin girls, who were at the same school as our two girls, and the children were best friends, so the parents bonded together. Andre was going to add a new room to his house, but I showed him how to make far more money by selling his house purchasing some vacant land down the road from me and building his own new home. For the same expenditure, he would quadruple his money the day the house was complete. That is exactly what Andre did, and they lived there when it was complete. One afternoon after grocery shopping, Mrs. Takis arrived home to find two black men inside. At a guess she would have shouted at them; to get out her house. The twins get home after school around 3.00 p.m. They could not find their maid or their mother, so they called their dad. Andre rushed home from work and called the police after searching for his wife. Her car was in the driveway and a few groceries were on the floor of the entrance of the home, so it looked like she had disturbed them. At 11.00 p.m. that night the police found her body at the foot of their property in some bushes. She was dead and had been beaten where no one could recognize her. This just a few doors down from our home, and there is no more prestigious location in all South Africa to live; than Lower La Lucia.

Another Murder:

This was in the newspaper. A couple of miles away in the outskirts of Durban, a man and wife had stopped off the highway for their little girl to relieve herself. Go potty, is the word most used. Two black gentlemen murdered both parents to steal their SUV and left the two little girls sitting on their parents' bodies, where police found them, hours later.

My dad had a friend who was a year or two older than me, and he joined the local police force in Umhlanga Rocks, which also covered Lower La Lucia. This gentleman's name was Ian. What a nice man; Ian often saw me during my visit to the little township of Umhlanga, and at times we would chat and others just a hi, depending on the day. One day he was chasing three local men who had broken into one of the smaller shops and stolen money in Umhlanga Rocks, and one of the men shot Ian in the left eye and Ian happened to live. The police caught the men and the newspaper hammered the police for beating the men. What do you expect newspaper reporter? Ian lived for six more years, then a blood clot from the eye killed him. Rest in Peace, good man. None of these were isolated incidents, and this was 1989, before 1994 when Nelson Mandela got into power. What a wonderful man. He was good for our entire nation, and he also strengthened the Africans who voted him in by opening the borders to everyone from Africa, and they flocked into South Africa to get jobs. When we left South Africa in 1990, there were thirty million people and five million were white. Today there are fifty-five million people and four million are white.

Necklace murders were common place on our front pages of newspapers. What is a necklace murder, you ask? If a local person steals a loaf of bread because he or his family are hungry, the group as a lynch mob punishes him by wiring a car tire around his neck, then filling the open hollow with gasoline and lighting the gasoline. The man runs around screaming for a few minutes and dies pretty quickly. Africa can be brutal. I also foiled a robbery to our home during the night in 1989.

In 1988, John Donnelley asked me to go into a large project with himself. He wanted me to bring in Arthur William's a friend of mine with a large net worth (a wealthy gentleman) who would be the major partner so the three of us bought a piece of land for one million dollars. John Donnelley had set up an idea to build twenty-four small factories because it had railway access and highway access and was almost in town. I did the plans at no cost, but John clearly said. "If this goes sideways you will lose your La Lucia home, and both Trans-Am vehicles." I signed as a partner and before building proceeded, John had sold half of the factories, off the plan. We completed that project and all three of us were pleased with what transpired, meaning the profit. My business life so far had moved along at great pace. I certain do relate good sport with good backbone and knowledge to do business. I was also at a disadvantage to other young men. My wonderful dad was an Army man, so no business ideas or plans were ever shared with me. My dad did share with me many honest, polite, trustworthy habits also to be on time for every appointment no matter what. "Be on time for all appointments no matter what." His wise words taught me the "I can do" rule, is more important than my 108 I.Q.

Good Advice to Your Son:

Integrity was all part of my upbringing. My dad called me Boy, and it was in a loving way. "The things you do under the cover of the dark of the night; will always be illuminated by the bright sunshine of the following day." He used to say that with highs and lows in the right places. It means if you steal, you naturally anticipate never to be caught, but you will be caught. If you do something that you are sure no one will ever find out, the future is waiting to show everyone, what you have done. All jailed prisoners thought they had got away with their crime, but the future got them caught and TV illuminated them. My dad had taught me to always be on time or make sure you are waiting at the appointment ten minutes before said appointment. Always be 100 percent on time or early no matter what.

Later in life, I was to read this next statement. The family are enjoying dinner one evening and the daughter Joan shares a rumor with everyone at the table. "Joan how do you know Patrick said that? Did you personally hear him say those words?" "No dad Hector Pollock told me Patric said that."

"Joan, go to your room and bring you pillow outside and meet me at the ladder outside."

Joan got her pillow and walked outside. Her dad said, "Okay, now climb the ladder to the roof." She did with her pillow. "Now take out all the feathers in your pillow and let the wind take them all over the place." She did this until all the feathers had been blown away by the wind. "I have no more feathers Dad." "Okay, now go and pick each feather up, and do not miss one feather." We all know that is impossible. The moral of this story is 100 percent correct

"A rumor is just as damaging as any fact, so in life do not spread rumors." I learned far more from my dad without knowing about business, I learned the basic backbone of business. Thank you, Dad. Our company motto for our clients has always been. "Our service to you today; is tomorrow's reputation"

This Is the Straw that Broke the Camel's Back: SATU.

One afternoon at 4.00 p.m. in 1989. I was on my way home from doing drafting alterations at John Peter clothing at the then new factory zone, and to get home, I was riding along the bank of the Umgeni River. This is a four-lane highway in and a new four-lane highway out of Durban. I happened to be behind a big green bus. The African buses were all painted green and their slang name was green mamba, like the snake. These green mambas were super big, so it was not possible to see around them, and this bus and I were in the fast lane headed into Durban. The green mamba started to slow down far too slowly and head for the slow lane to start to make a U-turn in the middle of this huge freeway. Immediate thoughts were crash ahead, so I also went to the grass verge hoping to ride around the crash. The bus did an immediately U-turn, heading out of Durban on the fast lane into Durban, but as the bus cleared, I had thirty Africans rush at my car. "We told you to turn around." I did notice many white cars across the road ahead of me, but my attention was with this large angry crowd. Had there been a brick or large stone nearby, I would have got that through my windscreen. I turned right behind the green mamba. I was as safe directly behind this huge bus. The bus was the very first vehicle to be subject to this problem and I was second, but now cars were screaming to a halt and tire smoke was billowing up all over the place. I kept right behind the bus until I saw a dirt road leading off the highway. This dirt road lead right through the Kwa Mashu township, and I eventually found a way back onto another highway leading back to Durban and La Lucia where I stayed. I had no idea what transpired but explained everything to my wife. Nothing in the night newspaper that night, but the next day, the huge head-line said that SATU (South African Taxi Union) had blocked the highway into Durban yesterday! The police had issued tickets to three taxi drivers for overcrowding passengers, bald tires and faulty exhaust pipes.

The taxi drivers would not pay their fine, so they were sitting in jail. SATU. Stated that all roads into and out of Durban (four million people) would be blocked until the three taxi drivers were let free with zero fines. I knew right there that when the masses demanded anything and the police force buckled, then our country was in for a very big problem. The masses were now in control. From that moment I made plans to emigrate to another country, and there were only two to go to. That decision as easy to make. England or the USA? England is cold. USA here come my family and me.

All of these rapes' murders, were getting far too close to home. I sat down with my wife to make plans to emigrate to the USA. At that time there were thirty million people living in Sunny South Africa 1990, with five million whites. We know Mr. Mandela opened all borders to everyone, once he was President (1994), which means today in 2018, there are fifty-five million people in sunny South Africa now with four million whites (just less than four million whites). Six percent of the population pays 100 percent of the government taxes, so today the country is in very poor shape and it is impossible to get better. In 1990 we could take out $500 maximum. This forced us to purchase a new catamaran and sail away to rosy shores.

I gave up working a four-day work-week in South Africa, plus owning one of the top luxury homes in South Arica. I did not have any doubts; that I would not flourish anywhere Gaile and I ended up. My character did not know failure. The reason for this huge upheaval was the turmoil in sunny South Africa. The future for my children and my grand-children had in South Africa, in 1990 was very bleak. Over the years, their future looks even bleaker, had we remained in sunny South Africa. The turmoil in happy sunny South Africa was now bleak and my mind made up when a taxi mob can dictate to the Police what they want done. We were now about to change countries. This is one huge undertaking, to start a new life in a new country where no one knows you is super difficult, but it unfortunately had to be done. America, here we come.

<u>1989 – 2019:</u>

South Africa was a nightmare with murders and rapes daily in the newspapers. 1989.

South Africa was riddled with upheaval, necklace murders were mentioned, too many other murders and rapes, just far too much upheaval were evident all-over South Africa. I am the captain of my family, this means I am the man of our family, and it is me who must protect my family. I decided to leave South Africa and to sail to America for a better life for my family line. I was working a four-day work- week, and my staff were all working on a Friday, so my business life and my home life were perfect. One of my pals said that I had built one of South Africa's top one thousand homes. That home today sold for six million and I had sold it for $750,000, It cost me $400,000 to build. Our home was also in the centerspread in the Sunday times, and that was a two-page full color spread. I sold everything and made plans to purchase a catamaran so we could sail to America. In those days the Government allowed us $500 to emigrate, so selling a catamaran in America would bring in more than $500 and it did.

This is where my sports success and business success elevated me. It is the success at sports and my isolated up bringing in Natal command had proved that leaving school in standard 8 (standard 10 in America) did not affect how well I was to do in life. I already felt like a success from all my sports life and then in my business life, so I had no fear of uprooting and going to America. I had no idea what I would do in a new country, but we were going. This proves that, "your can do" attitude is far better than your I.Q. The following is what happened in the next part of my life and at this time I was 47 years old.

I sold the architectural drawing office company I ran for twenty years. 1990 March From here I did not work, as I was waiting for our catamaran to be completed. We lived in St. Francis Bay, where in 1964 I had surfed the waves. We crossed the Atlantic and spent another ten months enjoying the Caribbean. We started chartering Splendidum in the British Virgin Islands.

THE CATAMARAN:

In early January 1990, we purchased the St. Francis catamaran, hull #-1. Yes, this was the first catamaran manufactured in South Africa by this new factory; called the St. Francis. I sold my architectural company for $100,000 and paid some $400,000 with extras for the catamaran. My plan was to follow John Donnelley in his larger catamaran across the Atlantic to the Virgin Islands and to do some chartering. Behind us were five other catamarans Shellette, Jungle Bells, Breanker, Quest and Bruce's. I was hoping all seven of us could leave Cape Town on the same day all head for the Caribbean. However, boat manufacture completion is not something one can predict, and all five catamarans were six months, or more behind John Donnelley in his catamaran named Tamarin fifty-seven-foot catamaran, and mine. We had to wait for our catamaran to be completed, and Tamarin was also to be completed at the same time as mine. Let's start with Tamarin, on the final day when John was going to pick up Tamarin a friend of mine needed hours in the air, so he flew me and another buddy up to Empangeni. When we were in the air over the harbor, we could see Tamarin and crew testing the catamaran, so we buzzed them and got real low to the catamaran where they were waving to us and us to them. We landed and then took a taxi to Tamarin, where we boarded her. Our plan was to sail that night and get her to Durban Bay at a dock so John could do final preparation for his trip down to Cape Town. John told me what transpired that morning when he arrived to pick up Tamarin. The boat yard was locked, and the owner said that he was short 100 thousand in debt, so John had no way other than give this gentleman and extra one hundred thousand and take his completed catamaran out of this yard forever and get rid of this gentleman. We were now on our own, and everything had gone well. All of us had our own beds in various cabins. We left the harbor in the dark early evening and I got sea sick, so I went to bed. I awoke the next morning and immediately knew something was wrong. Everyone was sitting inside not looking happy on this maiden voyage.

"Okay what's up?" I said to a puzzled group of adults. "Last night we lost both rudders, so we have zero steering and are drifting along the coast with the Mozambique current, just like a cork. Our radio is not working but we have tried to send out radio messages saying we are adrift. We doubt anyone will get them." "Okay, gentlemen so you are all going to sit here until it gets dark tonight and then start crapping yourselves. Has anyone hit the EPERB button?"

"No, we do not want John to get a bill for rescuing us!"

"So again, you are going to sit her until dark, and when it is dark all you guys are going to hit that EPERB button. We better do that now before noon, so we do have light to be rescued. Hands up to all who say yes to hitting that EPERB button!" and my hand went up with my statement. All hands went up.

"Okay so bring us that huge EPERB and lets gets this on the road." John depressed the button, and nothing worked. He did it again.

"Have a look to see if it has batteries??" (should have been checked before leaving shore). "OH no batteries!" So, we are dead with that one, but just then we heard a helicopter.

The helicopter came so very close to us they could hear us shout back to them. They asked, "Do you guys need help?" "Yes, we do." "Okay," over their bull horn, "we will get a tow vehicle to come from Durban to tow you guys home. Now prepare your catamaran with the largest rope you have and fix a bridle, ready to be towed." One hour later the tow boat arrived picked up our tow rope and towed us all the way home. That was the beginning of the Tamarin problems. Gaile (my wife) and I sold everything. I had one house being built in Empangeni through a builder friend, which was halfway complete, so my lawyer finished up with the builder, and five months later I was reimbursed for the house. Two other houses under construction when we left, I sold one, and my lawyer sold the second one. I had arranged to sail down to East London in South Africa on a mono-hull, and Gaile and both girls would pick me up by car in East London. Once in the car with my girls, we motored down to St Francis Bay, where the catamaran hull #-1 was being set up for her next step.

St. Francis Bay:

We rented a thatched cottage belonging to Duncan Leithbridge, who was the owner of the company manufacturing this new catamaran. Gaile and I were able to watch the build, as it was being done. We lived in St Francis Bay for eight months. Now twenty-six years later, after my surfing trip, I was back in St. Francis Bay with my family and not interested in any surfing. Gaile and I would go fishing in the river of St. Francis Bay. I would pump one-foot long worms and use the worms as bait to catch fish. I always said I married an Angel and Gaile has always been by my side no matter what I do; or did. If it was early morning fishing, she was there with me, rain or shine and when it did rain, Gaile was in her rain coat next to me. Our two girls had new friends their own age, so there was always something for them to do as well. Debbie worked at Bruce's surf shop and at a restaurant in the evenings. Susan would suntan and be the lazy one reading the odd book. Somehow Susan always attracted boys, and she was so casual about it. Ryan, the son of Lionel Donnelly, was locked into Susan; Lionel and I were good friends and Lionel was also the brother of John Donnelly. One Christmas Day, all the children, Lionel his wife, Gaile, and I were enjoying squid as prepared by Lionel, when Lionel took out fifteen Christmas-tree decoration balls and said, "Okay who-ever brings back the most balls will win a present". We were on the St. Francis canals and Lionel tossed in all these balls. Ryan and his brother plus two buddies were all big-time surfing men, so swimming is what they did daily. "Wait," said Lionel and the balls got blown by the wind in all directions and far from where we were standing. "Okay go." Susan, my daughter, dived in with all the kids and blew all of them away, she was faster by a long way, plus brought back the most balls. You go, girl.

The name Slpendidum:

Latin for Splendid. In 1970 1973 I used to keep marine fish in a tank, first at the apartment and then at our home in Sherwood in Durban. If you caught a Splendidum, you certainly were the main dude. We had caught Splendidums at Inhaca Island off Mozambique. I called my new catamaran Splendidum. This was a big mistake for chartering, because the name is a difficult one for Americans to hear for the first time, and it was also a name no one could remember. There were a few changes I did to the world of sailing without knowing it. Duncan Leithbridge was a very conservative gentleman and kept to tradition. I wanted sliding doors to the rear of my catamaran and insisted on the kitchen (galley) to be up. Having the galley up was a no-no in those days. Duncan insisted on having the galley below, but I wanted my wife as part of all action when she was cooking, so we did not lose her to below deck. I insisted and Duncan relented.

250 cc machine

1979

bike2

Andrew and Ian Brandon

In the pits with Rod Gray

Peter and I went away together a lot and here is a picture of my pal hurt after a 100 mile an hour crash.

Racing 750 cc motor cycles.

1958 soccer team the smallest gent on the far left was the top goal scorer.

the best band in Natal (the state of Natal south Africa 1961.

a 26 ft boat that sunk as it was tied to the Pier

Cannons under water in the Caribbean.
A real wreck was found by Andrew.

at 10 years old 1953 with Windsor Park school blazer on.

in Greece 1998 on board a charter yacht in Greece

My Home

Spear fishing in the BVI

This high-end picture of a catamaran in the Caribbean

This high-end picture of a yacht in the Caribbean

This high-end picture of crew, beach and water toys

This picture was used in the newspaper for the first Gunstan 500 surfing competition in 1965. Andrew in a curl.

SPORT: IS THE BACKBONE TO BUSINESS

THE Worst Night of Our Atlantic Crossing. 1990-1995

John Donnelley on Tamarin and I on Splendidum were now in Cape Town preparing for our Atlantic crossing. I had tried to get seven catamarans together all leave together, but all the other catamarans were too far behind us in being completely manufactured. Tamarin and Splendidum left Cape Town Harbor together December 31, 1990, as we passed Robin Island the sea was dead flat and calm so tomatoes and eggs were thrown at Tamarin, and they too reciprocated. The wind picked up during the night, and it was against the current making the troughs deep, but both catamarans were running with the wind; this is a very good thing. At midnight Tamarin was dragging behind us. At midnight they called us to say their eighty-five horse-power Volvo Penta in-board motor had nearly fallen through their catamaran to the seabed three miles below. They wanted to abandon ship. Our captain would not turn around in the huge steep swells.

He suggested both catamarans turn right and head for land with the nearest town being Luderitz. This is a very small coastal town on the coast in the middle of a huge desert. It was agreed to head across the swell to Luderitz. That night was the worst night we ever experienced in all our sailing. The waves were twenty to thirty feet high, with a little white water on top. The troughs were deep, and that is what breaks vessel structure. Sailing through such a night is what movies are made of, it is real scary stuff.

Our captain had put out our thickest rope we had on-board, and it was too slow down the catamaran from running down the face of each wave. Once we turned to run towards Luderitz, we were then running across the wave face. For a surfer, this is no issue at all. At 11.00 p.m. I had gone down to my cabin to sleep and was woken by a huge crash; I also nearly fell out of my bed. The crash was the washing machine falling out of the shelf it was on and other kitchen utensils also hitting the floor. I ran upstairs, and the captain had managed to get the boat back into play. The captain must have dozed off from lack of sleep, so I said, "Okay, go down and go to sleep, I got this." What had transpired was the nose of the catamaran had dug;

into the bottom of the wave, but it did pull out and that is what the crash and bump was all about. Both lines behind our catamaran also assisted with keeping the nose from completely submerging. Once I was at the wheel, all was good and slowly the morning arrived.

In the early morning we could see a mast two miles behind us and the waves were now much smaller. Both of us sailed into Luderitz, which has a ten feet tide change, so both catamarans ran onto the beach and anchored well into the sand, so when the tide ran out, we were both left high and dry on land. I knew this is where we were to leave Tamarin. Tamarin was to stay here for two years before getting back to Cape Town. I noticed large algae growth to my catamaran under the water-line, so within thirty days of launching, I already had underwater issues. We cleaned the hull as best we could, and within two days, we set sail for St. Helena Island on our way to the Caribbean. It took eight days and eight nights to reach St. Helena, where we stayed for two days, then hit the road for Ascension Island, which is an American satellite base in the middle of the Atlantic. It took six days and six nights to get to Ascension Island, and we could catch as much fish as we needed. Then we set sail for Recife in Brazil. We were so happy to hit a continent that I took everyone out for a slap-up dinner at the Recife marina restaurant. We docked the catamaran nose first to the cement dock and had to walk in three inches of water along the L-shaped cement dock because high tide was covering the entire dock in water. Our ladies were not happy, but we all wanted shore worse than a little water under our feet. After dinner we headed home. Now the tide was fourteen feet different to when we arrived, and our catamaran Splendidum was now perpendicular to the water level, almost hanging from both the nose cleats we tied to the dock. Lucky for me the aft was resting on a sand bar, which meant that the cleats on the nose of the catamaran were not pulled off my boat. All of us had to sleep almost up-right until the high tide resumed. We had crossed the entire Atlantic and had caught many fish, sail-fish, dorado and king fish, all too big to eat, while others just right. Now from Recife we headed to Natal, which was up a large river and again we stopped there for two to three days. Next, we headed for Fortaleza, also on the Brazilian coast, and we stayed in

SPORT: IS THE BACKBONE TO BUSINESS

Fortaleza for three days enjoying fishermen's fresh crabs and scallops. Now we headed past the Amazon 400 miles out to sea when a booby bird circled our catamaran and came to rest on our trampoline. We threw him bits of fish and he swallowed a piece or two. During the night, he made his way to the cockpit where we were on watch, and in the morning, he was comfortable with everyone on-board. One big problem he did those large white guano, that shot out three feet and the girls wanted him to go. This was a smelly, messy bird, but he was now friendly with all of us and we kept feeding him. It was agreed to let him go in Grenada.

Into the Caribbean:

Our first Caribbean Island was Grenada, and as we entered port, a rubbish collector had approached our boat in his tender, asking me to give him our collected rubbish. We did not have money to give to him because we arrived from a different country, so I said no, we did not need our rubbish collected, because we could not pay him. There were four large black rubbish bags on the rear deck, so he became annoyed and started to swear at me. I told him we had no money, and he swore all kinds of things to me. We went to customs and the bag man was there pissed, with us. Customs took passports and put them all into his top drawer. "Why did you not give your trash bags to the trash collector," I explained we had just come from Brazil and did not have Caribbean EC'S so I could not pay the man. "You from South Africa?" "Yes." "Okay, I keep your passports. Fill your boat with water, nothing else and leave within two hours, no provisions." We were hoping to relax for a few days but filled up with water got our passports and left Grenada. As it was getting dark, I shoved all four bags into the ocean close to the Grenada beach. They wanted our bags so desperately. Our captain was not impressed I had flopped the trash bags into the water. We stopped at many of the Windward Islands to enjoy, Horseshoe Barrier Reef. This snorkel was a great one to do because we snorkeled on the outside of this barrier reef and found a small nest of red sea-horses, which I have never seen since. I have seen sea horses in the sea grass and in various harbors, their colors were shades of light to dark brown, but never red. The water was crystal clear, and you could see for eighty feet in all directions. We did a short stop at Palm Island, and I was to meet the owner for a short period and remained in touch, see Johnny Coconut story.

Carriacou:

Cariacou was our first Caribbean Island after Grenada, and two miles before we entered the Tyrrel Bay, we spent one hour and; thirty minutes fighting my one and only black marlin and it was 141 pounds, I pulled it on-board and planned to sell it to a hotel on the island of Carriacou. We sailed into Tyrrel Bay and a local gentleman saw the huge marlin on the back of our catamaran and asked if he could buy it from us. I said sure, and he handed over the money. I had asked for the bill to be cut off and brought back to me, which I still have today. Try catching a black marlin the way we caught it, standing on the deck of our catamaran with a short seven-foot fishing pole, no harness, from pole to your body, no harness from your body to the fighting chair. Only now you know what it means to catch a big fish.

Horseshoe Barrier Reef:

We snorkeled on the outside of this barrier reef and I found a herd of small red sea horses which I have never seen ever again. I have seen sea horses in the sea grass and in the various harbors and all were shades of light to dark brown, but never red. At various snorkeling spots we saw squid, a shy snappy interesting creature, but the highlight were the red seahorses.

Palm Island and Johnny Coconut:

Palm Island after world war 11 was called Prune Island, it had bushy thorns and was a swampy, mosquito-riddled island; no one wanted. John and Mary Caldwell wanted to purchase their own island and Prune Island seemed Okay, so he approached the government of the day and bought the island for around $350 US dollars with a ninety-nine-year lease. John cleared the land and built a few small chalets to bring in some revenue. To make his island more popular he went around all the surrounding islands asking for coconuts that had shoots to them, and he planted these coconuts on his ground. John did this for many years and he became known as Johnny Coconut. Many times, over the years the government has tried to take the island away from John because today it is a gorgeous coconut-filled island with the name Palm Island. Smart man. Some years before Johnny Coconut passed away, he called me and asked me if I knew anyone who wanted to purchase Palm Island for five million dollars. John told me he wanted to leave one million to his wife and one million to each of his family. I did hear Palm Island did change hands, the St. James Club Group had purchased the island. A few years later John Caldwell passed away. Johnny Coconut did write a book called, "Desperate Voyage."

St Martin, Gaile Saves Two Lives:

One day we had four guests on board for a one-day charter. We took guests to a foot-print-free coconut- lined beach to enjoy, do some water sports, have an up-market meal on board with wine for guests only, and then make our way back to St. Martin. It was just after lunch and we were roughly six hundred yards off the beach going east, back to Phillipsburg Bay. I noticed a red racing buoy, sailors call a racing can. We have a racing can about two miles out to sea; Okay, we normally see these race cans when yachts are racing along a predetermined path, so I did not think any more on the red racing can. Gaile said to me, "Andrew that cannot be a race can because there are no yachts anywhere, let's go and take a look." So, we set off towards the red race can. As we got closer, we saw two gentlemen with red life jackets standing and waving at us. The bottom of their yacht was painted blue; What a big mistake, we would not have seen them if they did not wear their red life jackets, so to all boaters, always paint the hull of your yacht red. Okay we were coming. As we got close, I wanted to ask them to stay where they were until I switched off both engine propellers. The one man could not wait and jumped in and swam to my catamaran. Gaile took the helm and I went to the swim platform to lower the swim ladder, so the gentleman could climb on board. The man was up that ladder like a rat up a drain pipe. He grabbed my hand, his rings fell to the sea-bed one mile below and he locked his shaking body into the corner of our cockpit, shouting, "thank you," almost crying. He was so happy to be on-board and must have thanked us twenty times. The other gentleman I asked to tie a rope to his inverted yacht so I could tow it back to the shore. He did and then came on board. "Thank you, Andrew and Gaile. I have long since forgotten their names; Let's call them Bill and Chris. Bill was the smart one and here is his side of the story. Bill was telling us while we were traveling at one mile per hour, with the upturned yacht and sails, dragging behind us. We are Navy cadets and we asked to take the laser out for a sail because the day is so nice.

    The laser is a small thirty-foot sailing yacht with maybe one lower space in her hull, but the passengers sit on deck and have fun. We forgot to put in the plug, and we were going out to sea when the yacht started to sink below the water. We had our life jackets on, so we stood on the hull after she flipped upside down. One hour later we realized, we were drifting further away from the island of St. Martin. We were naturally waving at every yacht that passed but all were so far away from us no one came to rescue us. Then a speed boat turned and came to us when she was thirty feet he turned around and left us there. That is a crime when at sea. We have been standing on the hull now well over three hours, when you came to us. Christopher on several times wanted to swim ashore, but I managed to keep him on our upturned boat. I know that had Chris tried to swim three, or four miles, he would not be with us today. We eventually dropped both at their huge naval war-ship and untied their laser yacht. Months later Gaile got a letter from the admiral of the ship thanking her for saving their two lives and getting the yacht back to their ship. That letter I have in front of me and it is from the commander Michael Knowles, Royal Navy, HMS Ambuscade B.F.P.O. Ships. It reads, "Dear Mr. and Mrs. Buys, I am writing to thank you for your help and assistance in rescuing my two sailors and laser dingy which were in difficulties off St Martin. Undoubtedly your vigilance averted what was a potential disastrous situation, for the two people involved. Once again, many thanks for your help, fair winds and following seas for the future. Yours sincerely Michael Knowles. July 27." Well done Gaile.

Orient Bay:

Orient Bay is a nude beach; Gaile and I had been there once before with Keith and Meryl, the owners of Tiger Wheels, so we had seen Orient Bay. On this one occasion we did not go ashore we had simply anchored there for the evening, and we were by ourselves. It was early evening and I cracked open a brewski and Gaile decided to wash her hair and to take a shower, so off she went down-stairs to our cabin. I noticed a little black head sort of making its way to me at an angle, and it was normally people interested to see what a catamaran looked like. I did not mind showing people because in 1990 a catamaran was a novelty, something very different to a sailboat. As the black head got closer, I stood up and walked to the swim-deck and asked, "Do you want to come on board?" I noticed it was a lady and she nodded, Okay. As she got closer, I noticed she was totally naked, so I assisted her up the swim ladder and ushered her to sit down in the cockpit. "Do you want a beer," she again nodded. I went inside picked up a towel gave it to her, and she draped it around her. She took the beer and started to talk with a French accent, so we sat and spoke for a few minutes and almost completed our beers, when out walked my wife, Gaile. "Oh, I had no idea who you were talking to!" "How did you get here?" "she swam." I said and she is going to swim back. It's Okay, I'll drop her at the beach in the tender. So, my little naked lady and I got into the tender. She still had the towel around her, and I dropped her on the beach. She handed me the towel and we said bye, bye. I just had to answer a few questions and we got back to where we were, before Gaile went to shower for the day.

Martinique and Finding a True Ship Wreck never found before:

A real sunken pirate ship with twelve-foot cannons were found by me when snorkeling in 1991. When we arrived in Martinique, our captain and his wife had left the catamaran to fly home, when we were on the island of St Lucia. Left on board Splendidum was Gaile, Debbie, Susan, me and Ryan. It was us who sailed from St. Lucia forward. Gaile had slipped a disc, so we stopped in Martinique to fly Gaile home. Debbie wanted to go to Israel to the Kibbutz and Suzan wanted to fly back home to Gaile's sister Chloe, leaving both Ryan and me on-board Splendidum. The girls were gone, and Ryan and I were left on-board. We studied Martinique and noticed that the north-eastern side was marked with crosses and yellow on the world maps, meaning this is to shallow to navigate and is out of bounds for all ships. Okay, but we had a catamaran with a three-foot draft. We decided that is where we wanted to go so, we set of to go around the island to the other side. Slowly motoring across this out-of-bounds area, I noticed the depth gauge would drop to over one hundred meters deep and come back up to four meters within feet telling me the seabed had super-duper deep cracks that went down to oblivion. We tucked into a small anchorage for the evening and decided the next morning to do a lot of snorkeling. The next day was a perfect sunshine day and snorkeling began I was in twelve feet of water when I noticed the shape of a cannon on the seabed but it was covered by 250 years of coral growth except the end of the barrel where the cannon ball ejaculated from; that remained open and dark, so I knew I had found a cannon. Twenty feet further along was another cannon and then another, I had found five twelve to fourteen feet long large cannons laying on the top of a cliff face. It looked like each one had been carefully placed there. I also found three anchor chains two on each side of a major anchor chain. The major anchor chain had six-inch links and each link was five inches wide, the metal chain itself was as thick as my thumb, I place this down from memory, but this was links of a chain used in the 1700 s.

SPORT: IS THE BACKBONE TO BUSINESS

I snorkeled down sixty feet to find one of those very old twenty-foot-long olden day anchors. Both smaller anchors were round five to six feet long with small chain links. It was obvious what had transpired in the 1700-1710. A captain on his lage war-ship had been caught by a hurricane and had thrown all three anchors overboard hoping one of the anchors could hold and pull the nose of the boat pointing into the storm. It was obvious that none of the anchors hit the bottom and he was being pushed sideways onto shallow water. When all three anchors did catch, it was too later the entire boat with crew went down, to be found by Andrew Buys in 1991.

When Ryan and I left Martinique, I mentioned to the customs gentleman that I found cannons and ship wreck round the other side of the island. He asked me to wait, did a telephone call and said someone was coming to meet me. A few minutes later a gentleman with brief-case appeared in the door-way and asked me to show him where the cannons were. He pulled out a very large map of Martinique and I pointed to the spot. He said to me. "Mr. Andrew, we have no record of this, can you take me there?" I said sure, but I was not intending to use my personal catamaran to do that. He said, "No; He asked me if I could meet him at customs the next day at 7.00 a.m.?" I said, "Sure, Ryan and I will be there."

Ryan and I arrived at customs at 7.00 a.m. and lead to the tar road at the back of customs. There were seven customs vehicles and the last one was a large truck with a medium-sized speed boat on top. He said to me, "Mr. Andrew ride with me in the front vehicle and Rayna can jump into the next one." Both of us had brought fins and goggles. Okay, on with all the sirens and blue lights of all vehicles and we went down the road through different villages and to a beach on the far side of the island of Martinique. They launched the power boat and we piled in, "Now Mr. Andrew show us where this is." I kept pointing where to go, eventually reaching the spot, I said, "Drop your anchor here," which they did, and I jumped in with fins and mask so did the official gentleman. I pointed out one cannon and that was enough for him he was back in the speed-boat. "Mr. Andrew, thank you, this will in future be marked with a cross stating it is a ship-wreck. "Are you not going to do anything other than make a cross on a map?" "No." "So there is no reward for me?" "Ha, ha, no MR. Andrew."

Ryan and I had one interesting time, we sailed through the river Salee in Guadeloupe. There is a large harbor that closed into a small one-way opening bridge and the bridge only opens twice a day in the early morning and early evening. We waited for the bridge to open one morning, and we had ten inches on each side of our catamaran. Once through we notice a huge flock of white egrets and some had red feathers which I had never seen before.

Apparently, Guadeloupe birds had been sprayed with red dye when young. The Virgin Island Birds were sprayed gray and other white egrets sprayed blue, so that they could see how far and wide the white egrets flew weekly, monthly, and where they were going each day.

For the first time sailing we had gone from clear blue water to dark black water and both side of the river Salee had thick mangroves growing on both sides, and it was super shallow, but one mile later, we got back into the clear sea water. It was very refreshing to have this blackwater change to all the gorgeous turquoise water we had got used to. Guadeloupe looks like a butterfly on a map and is divided by the river Saline. The word *Guadeloupe* means 'butterfly.' Ryan and I were headed now to Antigua to enjoy the Antigua annual boat show and all the parties that happened every night. The sight of this annual boat show is always Nelsons dockyard and we had anchored just in the next anchorage, so when we went ashore, we were automatically part of the entire show, only we never inspected other yachts. Ryan and I were merely interested in meeting all the other yachties and drinking. Ryan was my daughter Susan's boyfriend, and he was a magnificent straight arrow gentleman, who I enjoyed as a buddy. I did have to watch his drinking and he never minded me placing him in check.

Ille De Saints:

Ryan and I did have one special adventure which was most unusual. We arrived in Ille de Saintes, and there are three islands which are exceptionally steep out the water and all three are volcanic, so a few roads lead up to a fort that Napoleon built, and this fort looked across at Josephine's fort he built on the opposite island. The small road also led to the opposite side of this one island. To get around you had to rent a scooter and pay the hourly rate as well as a refundable $100 damage deposit, so once this is all paid up front you hop on your scooter and you are gone. Ryan sat on the pillion behind me, so we visited the fort and went to the opposite beach. On our way back, we stopped at a five-foot-high tree with nineteen green iguanas sitting inside and on top of the tree. You could reach out to them and touch them, but you could see they felt we were in their space. On leaving I did a wheelie with Ryan hanging on for dear life, but as the small front wheel came down on the ground, both of us got spat off the scooter. Oh geez, the head-light had broken in many pieces and the bulging scooter side was well scratched and had a small dent, which was now much larger. Ryan picked up every piece of headlight glass and held them in his hand until we got back to the catamaran Splendidum. I got the press stick and some compound for the paintwork of the scooter. I put all the pieces of headlight glass together with this gummy press stick and polished all the paintwork. Now those scratches did not look glaring and the headlight looked good. We took the scooter back to the French gentleman. He inspected it all over, then gave us $100 cash. Ryan and I made our way back to our catamaran and picked up the anchor immediately and sailed for the next island.

After Antigua Ryan and I sailed back to Guadeloupe through the River Salee again; because Gaile was arriving back from her spine operation. Gaile had the disc ground away and has been perfect ever since. Ryan flew back to South Africa a few days before Gaile arrived. It was magnificent having Gaile back after forty-five days. The original doctor had said she may be away for six months. Thank God it was short and sweet, and she was her old self.

One of The Worst Days of My Life:

Well, not a good day at all.

We had a problem with one of our motors. The starboard motor (righthand side) needed a new head gasket. This was a small gasket as it only covered two cylinders, so it was not a big cost. I had to pay for the gasket plus shipping and this was done in Guadeloupe. The gasket would be with us in three days. The airport customs called to say the gasket was at the airport; I could go and collect it there. Bummer, every time you went somewhere, it cost $20, so I knew I was going to be out of pocket $20 one way and $20 back to the catamaran. Gaile and I picked up a local taxi and went to the airport. They wanted tax but could not find the gasket. They said they had sent it to the local BMW dealer, so here we go again $20, to the local BMW dealer. Years later, I think the customs was simply making me run around town because I was a South African. So Gaile and I arrive at the BMW dealer and we find the spares department then asked for the gasket addressed to me. They quote me $125 and said. "That is what the tax is!" Well, tell me that up front. Now I must shoot across the island and go to the bank to get an extra $125. And yes, again another $20 to the Bank, so I said, "No." Gaile and I would walk. Off we went, and the heavens opened to a huge down-pour. I was totally drenched, Gaile looked like a mouse; that has swum across a large river, and she was lagging far behind me; I was so angry with rain running into my eyes every two seconds, first one eye and then the other. We eventually got to the bank, and there was a line all the way out the building. It happened to be a Friday. I refused to stand in this line after what I had been through, so I asked, "Where is the manager?" "Sorry, no habla English, but the lady spoke in French. I asked the lady to draw some of my money; No English. I looked around and saw stairs leading up to the manager's door. I climbed the stairs, knocked on the door once dripping on the floor, and boldly walked inside, without waiting for acceptance. I was not a happy chappie; I was pissed I had wasted all the taxi money, and I was soaking wet. It was totally impossible to be wetter had I jumped into the sea with all my shoes and clothes on. There were three people around one large desk, and the manager looked up at me rather shocked, but he knew this was something different. Before I opened my mouth, drops of water ran down into one eye and two drops flopped onto his rug in his office. All of this happened in a split second. As I got into the office, all three heads turned around and looked at me, I was totally wet, I said, "Sir I am sorry to come to you, but I need to withdraw some money out of my account, and I cannot stand in a line leading out the building. As you can see, I have walked four miles in the rain to get here."

"Okay, can you wait down stairs for me" I said, "Thank you," and went down-stairs and waited possibly two minutes, then he took me to the end of the line outside and said, "Kindly wait here, and we will get you sorted out." I was not in his stupid line for three minutes when everyone disbanded, and they were closed for a two-hour lunch. We called another taxi and paid $20 again and simply went back to our catamaran. The taxi dropped us at the marina gate we were docked, and the lady at the marina office said, "Andrew your gasket arrived just after you and Gaile went into town today." No other monies were needed, they had simply made me run around the mango tree for their fun and games. This I only realized many years later. This day I should have been in bed, all day long.

Antigua:

Gaile and I headed to Antigua, where we stopped to charter with the Nicholson family, whom we got to know well. We had got to Antigua in April 1991 and anchored in the most gorgeous bay called Freeman Bay, which is just off Fort Berkley cannon point entrance, this links to Nelson's dockyard. Lord Nelson was stationed here during his life. Every July to October, the islands closes down all shops close and people just disappear, so we were left high and dry in Antigua all by ourselves. Only local islanders can spear-fish, so I never carried a float or rope when I went spear-fishing and always alone in super deep water. One day Gaile and I took our tender and went to anchor on a deep reef outside the St. James Club called Standfast Point, and it was here I speared the biggest fish ever. Once this was achieved, I never did spear-fishing again. I was thirty feet down and close to the end of my breath when a huge female horse-eyed jack (king fish in South African terms) swam across my path but well out of reach. Just behind her the male cut across the corner to follow her but he was just within range I stretched and pulled the trigger. The arrow hit above his spine in thick flesh, and I was very determined to hold on. Remember, there is only ten feet between the fish and the end of my spear-gun, and I was determined to spear my first large fish. I did not expect what happened next. The horse-eyed jack took off like a freight train at one hundred miles per hour, the spear-gun was held by both my hands. It was like a small tassel behind a charging hippopotamus and it seemed to last for many seconds. This initial charge by this Jack lasted about a good hundred yards. To slow him down, I wanted to provide surface area, so I held my arms above my head as high as possible, with the spear-gun adding surface area to him pulling me. To make this even tougher for this fish to pull me through the water so fast, I opened my legs as wide as possible. This was starting to slow him down, and after a few more seconds, I started to wave both hands from side to side, pulling the fish toward the surface, its direction changed he started to come up. I needed air sixty yards back, but now air was a serious aspect I needed. And I eventually broke the surface to take as huge breath, but that was short-lived the fish headed down again and again, I was being pulled along but not at the earlier speed. The fish was getting tired, and it soon breached the surface. I put my hand into his gills and called Gaile. Gaile could do nothing because the tender was anchored far below. I picked up my horse-eyed jack and put him in the tender. Then put the gun into the tender and went down to undo the anchor. I have a picture of my forty-one-pound jack that a gentleman took for me at the St. James Club. That is all I wanted, so I gave the jack to a local pal of mine who was delighted with his big fish. I had learned, when you shoot a large fish with the spear-gun and you only have ten feet of five-hundred-pound nylon strain fishing line. The impact the fish makes when it is initially hit, is so great, that the five-hundred-pound strain nylon line is snapped. I had this happen ten days prior and lost the spear when the fish swam away with it.

So, the first few feet at the end of the spear, I placed a rubber bungy style section with ten feet of heavy-duty woven wire trace inside the rubber bungy, so the bungy takes the initial impact of the fish blasting away. Now this worked to perfection with my horse-eyed jack. Never again did I spear-fish.

Once I had the picture of my one big fish, I cut the spear-gun down to a smaller spear-gun, to shoot lobster. The St. James Club is on the island of Antigua and where Martina Navratilova was the in-house tennis instructor.

Because everyone had left Antigua for hurricane season, Gaile and I decided to sail across to Barbuda. We arrived in Barbuda on the southern tip at Coco Point to anchor and just have fun. We went ashore to the hotel and not one soul was at the hotel, no guards, just no one we walked through that entrance hall and could see the large lounge. Everything was packed for hurricane month, which is September. We possibly stayed there one or two days and then headed for Captain Oliver's on St. Martin in the cozy bay of Oyster Pond. We made Captain Oliver's our home for a good few days. Captain Oliver's is a restaurant within Oyster pond, and we made great friends here. Our most memorable experience here was the woman had said, that men were not allowed to wear short pants for the next Saturday evening, we had to surprise the ladies. They meant they wanted their men to dress up in longs pants and lounge shirts. This last statement was not told to us men. The guys were talking about wearing white sheets with little else on, and other silly items. I have just had Keith Rivers from Tiger Wheels with his wife spend a week with us. I had designed their home in Umhlanga Rocks years before. Keith brought along two pairs of burry boasters. That is a thong swim costume for men. The thong at the back looked ridiculous and not too much hiding the front. I thought, Okay, I will wear the Thong swim suite, with T-shirt. Saturday arrived Gaile looked great as always, and I dressed in the almost naked scanty underpants called thongs for men. Oh boy, of course I felt a tad under-dressed, but all of us were adults and all were good friends with zero hanky-panky going on. We arrived and all the men had long trousers on (long pants). What the ladies meant was they wanted their men not to wear short pants, they wanted us to look smart. Oh boy, I had many of the wives pat my naked cheeks in appreciation and many a laugh was had. I could have changed but they kept me there.

Prickly Pear Cays:

one of the Caribbean's most out-of-the-way islands, not recommended for over-night anchorage. But we are different and not part of the crowd. In those days very, few luxury catamarans were around.

Gaile and I arrived at the Prickly Pear Cays in the early afternoon to see most of the day boats starting to go home to Anguilla, or St. Martin, and once that slows down the T-shirt vendors also go home for the day. Being a catamaran with a three-foot draft we can get into anchorages 95 percent of other vessels find totally impossible, so we anchored in this anchorage for the night. Gaile and I relaxed on the aft cockpit with beer in each hand and as the sun started to disappear behind the flat surface of the earth, to fall millions of miles somewhere, we noticed a small tender with a man rowing toward us. This happened a lot because catamarans in those days were most unusual, so I stood up to welcome them there was a lady in the tender was well. She stood up and said, "I am from Port Elizabeth as well." The back of our catamaran had the words *Port Elizabeth* (her home registered base) written on the back for all to see. I said, "The catamaran is from Port Elizabeth, but we are from Durban. Do you wish to come on board?" "Yes," was her answer, so we assisted them on-board, and both were given a beer to enjoy. The lady's name was Bridget Elliott. I cannot remember the gentleman's name. Bridgett is a gorgeous, blonde lady, and she had lived in Port Elizabeth, but she wanted to ask us if she could work for us as a stewardess. I said yes, but we were on our way to the British Virgin Islands and we would be there the following week. If Bridget found us in the BVI, then she could work for us, as we intended to do chartering. Up to now I had not worked since February 1990, and it was late September 1991. Living in the islands was killing me with no work and enough days of idleness. One-week later, Bridgett arrived on-board with a huge smile. "Andrew, I told my mother Pat Elliott that I had met Andrew Buys and Gaile Buys in the Caribbean, and I was going to work with them." Pat said to Bridgett, "I used to baby-sit Andrew, Dawn, and Dianne in 1955, when Andrew was 12 years old." Pat Elliott was also a gorgeous, easy-going blonde lady who was our favorite baby-sitter, and she lived down the road from us in 1955 remember it was now 1991. Pat asked Bridget to ask me if I wanted a picture taken in 1953 of the three of us children, she had kept in her album all these years. I said, "yes," and soon after that picture arrived. Thank you, Patricia.

British Virgin Islands:

The British Virgin Islands, and the impact the South African catamaran owners have had on this charter industry.

During snorkeling when you live on a yacht every day and snorkel every day, you get to go down deeper and deeper over the years and I could get down to sixty feet which to me was quite deep enough. We were at the famous Indians. I had two guests with me snorkeling and we were swimming around a large pinnacle called the Indians. I was normally at the head of snorkeling as a leader to point of Flamingo Tongues. This is a small white snail shell, but it lives with its leopard-colored spotted mantle covering the white shell as camouflage. If you touch the covering mantle, it withdraws the mantle, showing the glaring white shell. This is not easy to see with the eye unless you know what to look for. As I rounded the one end of the Indians, I saw eleven scuba divers coming towards us about thirty feet down, so I stopped my two guests and said, "Watch me, I am going to go down fifty feet, about ten feet below the scuba divers and at the same time I will round the corner fifty feet below. You to stay snorkeling on top of the water and watch." So, before I rounded this corner and knowing the scuba divers had not seen me, I went down fifty feet now, I was well below then, just with mask and fins. I casually rounded the corner looking at a soft coral leaf, looking in the opposite direction to the scuba divers, then turned and saw them and then went towards them, but far lower than they were, all scuba divers' heads turned my way and it took two seconds for them to equate. You could see by the look on their masks and body movement what they wanted to say. "Hey, this guy is down here below us with no scuba gear, what depth is he, what depth are we?" Half of them looked at their depth gauge and looked back at me. I casually went over to them and asked the one gentleman for air, and he shook his head meaning, no sir for you. There is a sign by cutting your neck with the right hand that tells the other dude, you need air. No, simply not, he shook his head, that told me he was a learner scuba diver, I think an established scuba diver, would have given me air. I went to the surface and the three of us cracked up. The shock on their masks, with their body movement, was so funny. Keep in mind there is no talking underwater, except by scuba signs.

Some British Virgin Islands History:

Robert Louis Stevenson's three famous pirate caves in his book, is taken from these three caves on Norman island, which is in the British Virgin Islands. All our lives we thought these to be fables, but many stories are British Virgin Islands history. The island was called Norman Island after a local gentleman called norman played a trick on some pirates in the late 1700's. This pirate ship had gone aground around Anegada, a coral atoll. The pirate captain wanted a location to hide his treasure which was on-board. They were busy taking the goods ashore and placing everything on the beach. Norman a local gentleman said he knew the correct place to do this, plus the place was also close to the local town on the major island of Tortola. So, the captain and Norman with the goods were placed in Normans fishing boat, and they went down to the now Norman Island and hid treasure in one of the caves. I do not know what happened next, but I have read that treasure was really found in cave number three in late 1800s, or early 1900s by a fisherman taking shelter from the rain. Looking up the fisherman saw a leather pouch protruding from a crack and pulled it out to reveal treasure.

When snorkeling at all three of these pirate caves, the charter yachts, pick up a buoy. Then all guests and their captains slide off the rear swim platform and into the warm body temperature crystal-clear water to snorkel. One buoy was in deeper water than normal. Robert Young and I got into the water to snorkel these three caves, and as I looked down at the seabed some forty feet below, I saw a green dollar bill. I took a deep breath and went down, and as I got close to the dollar bill, I saw it was a twenty-dollar bill, I picked it up and rose to the surface. Ha-Ha, $20 for spending. The caves are unique in all the islands because you can snorkel in super-clean warm water and the sunlit water turns to dark shaded light but you can see well into the back of each cave, plus there is no growth on the rounded rocks on the floor of the cave, so you can stand up in three feet of water. Then swimming back into the bright sunshine just at the mouth of each cave is another neat experience.

We have all heard the fable: "Yo-Ho-hum, a bottle of rum, twelve men placed on Deadman's chest." Apparently as punishment Blackbeard placed twelve men on Deadchest Island with one bottle of rum to die. One had tried to swim across to Peter Island and got washed up dead on the beach, so today the bay is called Deadman's Bay on Peter Island. This apparently is British Virgin Islands history.

Murder: A German gentleman and his wife rented a power boat for the day, and both were relaxing on-board he went down to do something in the cabin, and when he returned, his wife had rolled over the top deck into the water, but he did not hear anything. Her body was never found. The police did a search and found two shoes belonging to the lady together on the beach. This by itself is suspicious because if her shoes also went over-board, which the husband said she must have, the shoes would never be together. There is a seven-thousand-foot drop-off one mile from Peter Island, so if a ladies body was weighed down and thrown overboard, it would be impossible to find her, so far below. We never heard an out come to that one.

The British Virgin Islands is known for its beauty. The baths are a must-see location when anywhere near Virgin Gorda. The baths were formed and named by forty- and fifty-feet large boulders assembled around this one spot. Red hot liquid lava spewed out of the earth, and when it hit the atmosphere this liquid granite solidified, all coming to rest half in, half out of the water, well up the beach and many on top of each other. The small pools between these balancing boulders formed were called The baths, hence the name, the Baths. In 1994 the government paid a few young men and women to make wooden stairs; between these boulders, and today some twenty three years later, those same stairs remain at the baths. The head gentleman sailed with Gaile and me after they completed those wooden stairs. The reason for the stairs is so that more guests can walk across to Devil's Bay, which is one gorgeous bay. Named Devil's Bay because smugglers use that bay at night to drop their products, under cover of darkness. The name was given many years ago, but it remains today.

When Gaile and I first started out, we were following Tamarin and John Donnelley, but Tamarin was a nightmare and ended up in Luderitz on the west desert coast of Africa. We had also tried to leave Africa, with Quest, Shellette, Breanker, Jingle Bells and Bruce's. That did not work out. Shellette arrived in the Caribbean six 6 months after us, then 3 years later, Breanker and Quest arrived, all going to the US Virgin Islands. Gaile and I on-board Splendidum, were the one and only catamaran in the British Virgin Islands for two years before another catamaran arrived and her name was Take-Two. Lavity Stout was the head of the British Virgin Islands, and in my days there we had to meet Mr. Lavity Stout personally, and we did our interview, so in those days, it was he who allowed us to trade in the British Virgin Islands.

Catamaran chartering has impacted the growth of chartering by eight or nine times the size chartering was, in those days. Almost every catamaran was a South African catamaran, but the French from Guadeloupe soon realized that they needed to be based in the BVI. The British Virgin Island locals are the nicest people to know and this is my personal experience, always charming and always there to assist us when needed. I have heard recently one or two South Africans have tainted the image we have set, but it always takes one; or two characters to mess things up. The customs and immigration folk take no prisoners, and hopefully the bad eggs will be weaned out. Chartering comes with many varied stories; All our guests almost without exception were exceptional people. We had a Spanish couple who had just been married, so they were on their honeymoon. When they first boarded Splendidum, she asked me in broken English to tell her when to put on her swimming top and when to take it off. Okay with me, and I named her, "toppy on and toppy off." When we arrived at a marina I would say, "Toppy on." And her puppies would be hidden from the world. When we snorkeled, that top would be taken off and I would join them. Someone had to show them the way to go. Great charter.

In 1994 a catamaran company had one of their catamarans sail from St Martin to the British Virgin Islands, and that is the better way to cross that 111-mile open ocean passage. This passage is normally done commencing at 5.00 p.m. to the next morning, so your arrival time is when there is light. At 1.00 a.m. the captain notices the boat had hit something with her starboard hull, and water was gushing into the two cabins. Not good so he ordered his crew to call for help S-O-S. They abandoned ship and their catamaran moved away from them in their small tender. He was picked up by the Virgin Island Search and rescue, and they were in their life raft (or their tender). They had abandoned ship and were Rescued. The motors were running on idle when they left the catamaran, so it toddled off into the distance before the VISR reached them. The next day they were safe and back at their office in Tortola. But catamarans cannot sink. This we know, is a fact, so why did the captain abandon a good ship? The owner rented a small aircraft and decided to go and look for the catamaran with the captain. They found their limping catamaran doing huge circles in the open water with it still idling, one side heavy with water from the night before and the other side happy as can be. Maybe the captain did not realize his ship could not sink, or he panicked. Their catamaran was towed in repaired and was back in the fleet a few weeks later.

BUCANEER:

Mike Mitchell and Debbie ran a charter yacht called "Dollar Corn." Mike gave me the biggest Buccaneers football orange flag to hang off the mast of my catamaran, which I did for a few days. We used to pass each other with charter guests on board both our catamarans and I would shout across to him in passing, "Where are your Buccaneers?" and his reply would be, "On my buccan- head." Well that would always get a laugh. Today when I see him twenty-six years later, we still get a kick out of that. Men can be men. The name of Michael's boat Dollar Corn has a great story behind that name.

The owner of Dollar Corn, asked his wife if he could purchase a sailing yacht and she said, "Yes as long as he did not name the boat, Buccaneer." "Okay honey I will not name the boat Buccaneer." He called his yacht Dollar Corn. Let me break that down. Buck, equals, Dollar, and ear can be called the ear of corn, and so the name developed. Dollar Corn. The most hilarious name of a yacht I have seen was docked in the mouth of a river, that opened out sea. The name was "Sir Roses of the river." Now say Sir roses of the river, five times, as fast as you can, and the laughter should follow.

Common sense:

Two couples had rented a twenty-five feet day-boat from a company called the Naughty Nymph. These day boats can be rented to anyone for the day and these four people had rented this power boat to view different islands. So, they set off into the British Virgin Islands and in the middle of the channel, they realized their boat was taking on water badly. The Sir Francis Drake Channel is 5 miles wide with islands all around, so you can always see islands. Not knowing what to do all four put on flippers and mask so if they had to swim, they would. Not a smart idea. Many various vessels went past them as no distress calls, or waving had been done by anyone of the four, which meant that no one picked them up. Then an eighty feet power boat captain wondered why four people would have their feet in the water, with masks on in the middle of the channel, so he went past very slowly and asked, "Can I assist in anyway?" "Yes, please, our boat is sinking." "Okay, throw me a line and I will see if we can pull you and your boat to shore." So, the towing began, and it took twenty-three minutes to get the boat to an uninhabited part of Peter Island. They managed to get to Peter Island where there is an unused dock and as they tied the boat to this dock, the boat finally sunk. I have a gorgeous picture of this boat on the bottom tied to the unused dock, in crystal clear water it is very clear to see.

The Fish Trap:

The Fish Trap was a new restaurant that a gentleman, and his family opened in Road Town, but it is no longer there. When off charter, we used to go to the Fish Trap on a Friday night and, have beers and a great home-made dinner. They were very popular and used to put out a few plates of free tasty chicken wings on the bar counter. I would normally bring a plate to our table, give everyone one and take the plate with a few wings back, and leave that on the bar counter. One evening, Gaile and I got in a tad later than normal. We sat down with a few friends at a table and ordered our beers. The bar counter was full of men waiting to be served, and I wanted to see if the chicken wings were still on the counter- top, but there were far too many men in the way. I walked closer and could see the top of a plate with what looked like wings. I slide my hand between two men and took two wings, one for Gaile and one for me. Just as I got back to where we were sitting, I saw a look on my wife's face. I tried to hear what she was saying. "You took those wings from a man's dinner plate." What I turned around to see a gentleman turned around looking at me but a definite smile on his face. Oh dear, I realized what I had done. I walked back to him. "Sir I will happily buy you a fresh plate of food." "No, it's quiet all right no harm done. I insisted, and he assured me it was fine, so I enjoyed one wing and gave Gaile the other. I do get into the odd embarrassing issue; in this case, we had a charming understanding gentleman.

Every Story in This Book is True:

Since 1995 I have been on Dilantin and phenobarbital medication for secures. I was in Durban ready to get back to the British Virgin Islands to the catamaran and to Gaile, my wife. I had a two hour lay-over in Johannesburg on my way to the Caribbean. My sister Dawn lived in Johannesburg with her charming husband and her daughter. Dawn called and said, "Andrew I will pick you up at the airport when you get to Johannesburg and take you to my home, you can have a bath, then dinner and I will get you back in time to the airport." "Dawn, that is far too little time I just see me missing the plane back to New York." "No, I promise to get you back in time." "Okay, but I need to bath, I have not shaved or had a bath since yesterday.' I arrived in Johannesburg and Dawn was there, so we shot off to her home and sat down for dinner but talking just got the better of all of us. "Yikes, look at the time we are already late." So Dawn and I raced back to the airport. Wonderful time but no bath, no shave. I had white longs on and a blue anorak (hoodie). As I ran past the wine store, I stopped and bought my wife a white and a red South African wine she loved, one in each pocket of my hoodie, and onto the plane I went. I always get the window seat, and next to me were a very young couple just starting their honeymoon. We had dinner on-board again, and I realized I had left my pills in the overhead bin. I did not want to irritate the couple, so I decided to go to sleep. At 11.00 p.m. I fell asleep. I opened my eyes and I was in a room with bright fluorescent lights all-around and nurses. I was in hospital; the time was 5.00 p.m. the following day nearly twenty hours later. I was on a gurney near where the nurses sat out their shift. "Andrew, you had a seizure." said some nurse. There is zero warning that this is going to happen, but when you start to come around, it takes three or four days to get back to normal. Your thinking is slow, and your talk is slow and sometimes a little slurred. I was still in the same clothes now with a growth of beard. I had puked on one leg of my white long pants, both bottles of wine remained in my blue hoodie, and I had zero teeth, the top and bottom plates had fallen out and lost. "Nurse, please get me a taxi, my wife must be worrying where I am." I had left Durban twenty-four hours ago and have not bathed for 48 hours. The bathing part never entered my mind, getting to the airport did, because I knew my wife would be very worried. A taxi arrived and took me to the airport and must have asked me if I had eaten and was I hungry I must have been, because he took me to a New York restaurant I do not remember the discussion, or the restaurant. I was sat down and eat a wonderful plate of food, then off to the airport where I said goodbye. I have no idea if he was paid or not. The hospital should never have let me go in that state. I arrived at the airport desk and put my hand on my mouth with no teeth and said.

"Excuse me, ma'am, I need a ticket to get to the BVI." She said to me, "Go away." "No, ma'am, you do not understand, my wife is waiting for me in the BVI." "Go away, or I will call the police." "Okay, I am going to sit here until you give me a ticket." And I sat right in front of the lady, waiting for her to be civil. A few hours later the lights went out and the lady was gone. I sat in the one chair all night. During the night, I went to use the urinal and fell on four steps, breaking the red bottle of wine, so now I had puke all over my left leg and red wine all over my entire right leg of my white long pants. The next morning a new lady opened American airlines, and I walked to her and put my hand over my mouth to hide no teeth. I must have really looked like a bagman from the streets.

"Excuse me ma'am, I need a ticket to get to the BVI, my wife must be worrying about me." "Have you got a ticket sir?" "Yes, Ma'am." "Where is it?"

"In my pocket."

"Okay then, hand it to me." So out comes the ticket and I handed it to her. Just by this one movement of going directly to my one pocket, tells you I knew where it was, but I was unable to think of the ticket. "Oh geez, Mr. Buys, your wife has been calling to find out where you are." "Gaile your wife, is already on her way to Puerto Rico to back-track and see where you are." I never carry a telephone. I was on the next plane down to Puerto Rico, and as I walked out the door, there was my wife in Puerto Rico. She knew I would be there, because they had contacted her to tell her I was on that flight. She said I smelled *so* badly, it was now 72 hours since I had a bath, or a shave, plus I was covered in wine and other smelly stuff. My wife found my teeth in one of my pockets of the hoodie, and I still had not got back to normal. Looking just like a hobo from living under a bridge for one year does not make one a hobo. Looks can be deceiving. A big thank you to that kind taxi driver and to the kind restaurant owner for the food. I wish I knew who you guys were, so I could reward both of you.

The Pelican:

I have a U.R.L. for this story also with pictures. http://www.yachtingbase.com/yachts/pelican/

While Gaile and I were chartering in the Caribbean learning all the anchorages for our guests, we used to take these free weekends with friends and get lost in paradise just chilling out. Gaile (my wife of forty-nine years) is one of those wonderful gentle folks who people, dogs, cats, and birds, are attracted to. When we were in the Virgin Islands those single girls would gravitate to "Mother" Gaile, so there was forever a bunch of single girls hanging around our catamaran and the safety of Mother Gaile. One July weekend in 1993, the girls decided to rent eight movies and then we would find a quiet anchorage where we would hang out for the weekend. We found our anchorage off Peter Island called little harbor. After snorkeling most of the morning, the six girls and I were sitting on the trampoline when I realized that water is heavy. There were many pelicans diving for minnows around our catamaran, and it struck me that for two- or three-seconds pelicans are unable to fly, when their pouches were full of water and small fish. Their pouch holds about three pints of heavy seawater and small minnows, so they purge the water out of their beaks tilt their heads and swallow their catch. This meant they were vulnerable to being caught by hand, provided one dived near our catamaran and I could time it exactly correctly. If I ran off the side of our catamaran and dived in the air, just after the pelican hit the water, close to our catamaran, I would then flare open my arms and catch the pelican with a beak full of water and fish. "Girls what would you bet me, if I can catch one of these pelicans flying around us, with my bare hands in the next few minutes and you can touch the feathers, then I would let it go? Eeeeeugh what are you talking about, they all said in total disbelief, impossible. "OK we have one slab of chocolate for the whole weekend we would bet you the slab of chocolate." I do not remember what I promised them if this did not work, I did not tell them how this was going to go down anyway. I sat and waited for the right pelican to fly just too close to our catamaran, while I was waiting, they were teasing me. "So where is the pelican

Mr. Hot Shot??" "Wait," I said, and they teased me even more. I waited, all the time watching. Ten minutes went by with constant heckling by those female nonbelievers, then the right pelican was within the distance I felt would work. I was running along the side of the catamaran and just behind the Pelican, then I dived into the air, (I was diving). The pelican hit the water a second before I did. I hit the water far enough away from him, not to hurt him but to come up after the initial underwater dive right where our Mr. Pelican was. It was too late for Mr. Pelican as he emerged with water and fish in his beak, I surfaced right next to him with open arms. His wing span was far too big to get him moving in time to escape my closing arms. His beak remained full of water and little fish, this pelican was surprised, but nowhere near as surprised as six women sitting on deck in total disbelief. Then there erupted the loudest laughter ever emitted by any female, and there were six of them. They were cracking up on deck, tears running down their faces, and two wet the deck. I had to stop them and say, "Go and get a camera, ladies, I cannot stay here all day waiting for you to take these pictures." So, the pictures you see were taken by those non-believing ladies on deck. This story was also featured in the Virgin Islands newspaper, but they added a touch by calling the pelican Penelope. So Captain Andy caught Penelope, but it was a male pelican.

Mell Jacobs: Mell Jacobs is just a different man to all other men Mell had a passion to sail, so he sold his farm in New Zealand and bought an eighty-five-foot three-mast sailing yacht named Classique, and then he got to work to sail around the world. His wife and family had no plans to do this with Mel, so he worked on his second hand large new yacht by himself. Mel's working hours were always 6 am to midnight, catch a few winks, and back at work at 6.00 a.m. again to fix his yacht ready for his trans-world cruise. Mel was not a man to spend one cent of his money, he rather made substitute parts himself, or worked around an issue. One day a lady by the name of Carol asked if she could work on his boat with him. Now Mell was around forty-one years old and Carol was around twenty, so Carol was like a daughter to Mell. Carol could also be called his slave. "Yes, Carol, you can work with me on-board, but there is no money to pay you. "That's fine, I just want to work on a yacht." Carol also got into the midnight to 6.00 a.m. working hours. Once Mell was ready to do his first small leg of this cruise, he had to sail from Perth to Darwin. This one-thousand-mile cruise he did by himself, after which he would leave Australia. Carol begged Mell to let her also go on the first leg of the trip to Darwin. "No Carol, this is where we say good bye and thank you." Mell did the trip by himself and arrived in Darwin, only to find Carol on the dock waiting for him. "Bloody hell Sheila, what are you doing here?" "I want to come with you around the world and my parents gave me a note to give to you, allowing me to be on board!" "Okay, no pay Carol, let's get to work." "So, for the next week, Mell and Carol hit the road running their hectic pace getting this huge sailing yacht ready to cross the globe. Eventually Mell and Carol set sail and headed well into the open ocean and into the middle of the sea. Eight days out Carol sat down with Mell and told him that she had cancer and it was at stage four, and she had pestered her parents to let her do the trip. Three weeks into the trip, Carol passed away, and at the first stop Mell contacted her parents and told them her body was at the island he had just reached. So sad to hear, but life has many twists we do not expect. Mell carried on by himself and had one mast break during a storm which he jerry-rigged himself. Mell arrived in the British Virgin Islands where I met him, and he and I became dear friends. Gaile and I knew he was always alone in that huge yacht, so I often asked him to pop over and have a beer with us. One evening just as the sun went below the horizon, I saw this Hobby Cat slowing zig-zagging it's way to us. It was Mell in his underpants (those underpants did not fit well) with two beers to share with us. He wanted to save gasoline money, so sailing over did the trick. In all my life around motors, I have never seen a motor like Mell's motor on board his huge yacht. There were oil leaks, wires holding joints together string holding pipes in place, and rags wrapped around pipes, but it worked just fine for Mell. Spending money was not what Mell did. Mell started to do one-week yacht charters to make money. He would take out six or eight guests for one week to explore and enjoy the Virgin Islands. On one of these charters, my daughter Debbie was the stewardess on-board. One evening during their charter the guests asked for more wine. Debbie went to the wine storage and took a nice bottle out of storage, Mell saw her and asked, "What are you doing with that wine?" "The guests asked for another bottle of wine," said Debbie. "Tell them the wine is finished and put that bottle back." That from Mell, Debbie did as was told, and placed the wine back in storage. She then told the clients the wine was finished. The guests bought their own wine the next day. Mell put an advert into a local American newspaper looking for a lady partner of a yacht in the Caribbean. The investment asked for a sixty-thousand-dollar investment as partnership, and Mell got a few calls. The call he accepted was from a blonde lady who had saved sixty-thousand-dollars, and she agreed to the terms, with her long painted finger-nails. In her mind she was going to laze in the sun on her yacht dreaming the sunny days away with Mell. To Mell she had to do the cooking of three meals each day plus fixing the yacht and sailing the yacht with him. So, both parties were miles apart from day one. We will call the blonde lady Vivian. Mell banks the sixty-thousand-dollars and no one is getting that back. The first few days were perfect, then their first charter together was coming up in four days and Mell told her to go and purchase everything for the charter. "No, thank you." and she disappeared to a hotel until the charter was over. Vivian came and complained to Gaile and I about giving Mell her sixty-thousand-dollars and she did not cook. Gaile explained it was easy and after the fourth or fifth charter she would be well in the grove. "Oh, no, that is not what I paid for. We said sort it out with Mell. The next night Mell sailed over in his Hobby Cat. "Gee Andy I have a problem. Every time a charter comes along, Vivian runs away and pays for a hotel for the duration of the charter, she just will not do any cooking." "Mell you simply have to work it out with her. By the way, are you still sleeping with her?" "Geez." a very sheepish-looking grin formed on Mell's face. 'Yes, I am." "Oh well, Mell. "This is a problem you are compounding." I do not remember what happened to Vivian, but she did eventually fly back to the USA, left Mell and the yacht named Classique.

President Carter: This from Doug and Mary with their three children on-board a sailing charter yacht named Blackfoot. Doug and Mary have a few hairy stories to tell about their time on-board and off-board Blackfoot. The one that sticks in my mind is this one about President Carter. Doug and Mary with their three boys were sailing up the Intercoastal Waterway. They had started from Fort Lauderdale and were headed toward New York to stay with friends. One evening Doug looked for a good spot to be out of the way to night traffic, so he turned into a small tributary and tucked away for the evening. It was a great night stars out and early to bed for their next leg the next day. After breakfast, Doug pulled up the anchor and headed back to the Intercoastal Waterway, the I-C-W. As he reached the ICW he swung left and headed north one again, it was Around 11.00 a.m. and a gorgeous sunny day, but there seemed to be something different. Normally the Intercoastal has traffic up and down no matter where you are. The water is always dead flat because you have land on either side of this natural canel stretching from Miami all the way to New York and many bridges to cross under. When you are on-board a yacht the days blend into each other so, "It must be a Sunday," is the first reaction Doug had. Doug was close to the left-hand side of the ICW, when suddenly, out of this quiet morning he heard his son shouting and waving both hands on the front of Blackfoot. "Hello, President Carter, hello, President Carter." he turned to his Dad and said, "Dad there is President Carter." He turned back shouting, "Hello, President Carter, still waving both hands. "Stop shouting son!" and the son quietened down. President Carter was giving a talk to troops and was standing on a high podium in front of a pavilion and Blackfoot was so close they could clearly see the president and the President turned. Out of the blue came four-armed Coast Guard boats were bearing down on Blackfoot, these boats were coming from all directions. Doug slowed to stand still, and the coast guard boarded them guns out from the first time Doug saw them. The children were scared stiff, the first words were, "What are you doing here sir?" "We are just cruising up the Inter Coastal Waterway." "We closed that off two miles down and 2 miles above this point, how did you get into this area?" Firmly and aggressively by the man on board. Doug answered, "We spent the night at the turn-off about a mile down river sir." "We checked that spot captain, no one was there." "We were there sir, and I had no idea you had stopped traffic over this section." It was established that Doug Mary and the wide-eyed kids were little threat to safety, so the Coast Guard gave them an escort to the outside of the zoned area. Once outside all three kids said, "Hey Dad that was cool. We saw President Carter, yahoo."

One More Blackfoot Tale:

Doug and Mary had decided to build a small house themselves with assistance on a small piece of ground they bought in Belize between coconut palms on the beach. They had got almost complete when a huge hurricane hit them. Blackfoot was anchored somewhere in Florida many miles away, and they went to high ground as the wind started to pick up. Doug dug two large depressions so that their bodies could fit into and their water and food was next to them. They also had a dog that was right next to them. The wind picked up 100 miles per hour, 120 miles per hour, then 150 miles per hour, and the hurricane stalled for two days, and then to 180- miles per hour. During these strong winds they did not venture outside their hole in the ground they were in. The dog was shivering most of the time. Doug and Mary thought they were going to perish, the wind below right over them, all the coconut trees were stripped bare and all their hard work was for moot. Nothing was left, they did survive but only just. This was the same year one of the large sailing ships went down in the Gulf of Mexico with all on-board. Doug gave me a short description of sailing: Sailing is 95 percent total pleasure and 5percent sheer terror. Thank you, Douglas and Mary Solomon, on Blackfoot.

Russian Eggs:

I did hear one serious true story by one of my friends who were on board a 172-foot power boat when this true tale developed. The yacht is a super-duper expensive yacht that millionaires rent for one or two weeks and do not feel the pinch. Five Russian couples headed by Mr. B. Pulkeska rented this 172-foot private luxury yacht for twelve days and they were in the Galapagos at the time. The women (the wives) were running around naked and the men were all almost naked as well and the crew were okay with this, but it was their attitude towards the crew. "Slave, get me a pink Russia and now," was the demand, "no please," or "thank you." Even the women were nasty and demanding. They would get up at different times in the morning demanding breakfast. It was a tough charter. One morning boiled eggs were ordered and served to the guests and Mr. B. Pulkeska noticed the eggs were one day out of the expiration date. He stood up and whipped his hand across the table slapping his egg and others onto the floor stating, I don't eat eggs out of date. The captain tried to explain that food in the Galapagos normally came in from other countries and they could not get any more eggs, plus one day out is no issue at all. We do not eat expire food. All the staff were tiptoeing for the rest of the day, plus they still had seven more days to go on charter. At 1.00 a.m. that next morning the telephone on-boat the yacht rang, and it was Russia asking to speak to MR. B. Pulkeska. The captain told Russia he was not going to wake up Mr. Pulkeska. The voice on the other end in Russia said. "You better go and get him right now, because his business partner had removed all his money from his bank account, and he was totally ruined." The captain knocked on the door, and a rugged voice said, "I sleep, do not wake me." "Mr. Pulkeska it is Pavel Hetrovka on the line and says your business partner has emptied your bank account, he wants to talk with you now." Naked he answered the telephone and told the captain to get him and his party to the nearest airport, and wake everyone up now. And so, this charter ended, no refund, plus they were now off the yacht.

The Most Gorgeous Sight in All My Caribbean Snorkeling:

I had got very used to snorkeling in fifty and sixty feet of water all by myself, remember there generally is no one else to enjoy some of these sights in the middle of the week, when I was off having fun.

I had gone to a spot I had never been to in the past and never happened to go there again for no reason. This is an out of the way scuba buoy spot, east at the far end of the three pirate caves on Norman Island. I tied my tender to the buoy and the water is round twenty-five feet. I slipped into the water and snorkeled to the deeper water because it was noon, on the best sunny day of the year, the water was gin clear and you could see eighty feet in all directions plus the water was dead calm. I noticed a spotted eagle nose ray with his/her twenty-foot-long foot long tail standing dead still, about fifteen feet below the surface. This Stingray was out stretched as if to catch every ray of the sun, it did not move and that tail was horizontal to the surface, so I wanted to see how close I could get to this gorgeous beast. I snorkeled down to fifteen feet and very slowly made my way closer to the Stingray, closer and closer, gosh this was a magnificent sight. It was if the Ray was motionless in the air just looking around and enjoying what she/he saw, plus I was on her/his radar and vision, as I got into its space she flipped away and was like a bullet one hundred yards down the line in one or two seconds. Wow, that sight has always remained etched in my mind. The beauty of nature. Have you ever thought how the gentle, sensitive stingray got her name? Fishermen many years ago used to catch rays, like we do today and once out of the water, they take their knives and stab the poor creatures in the back to kill them. To defend themselves, the poor ray arched its back and tries to stop the stabbing by protecting itself with their long-pointed stinger on their back. Hence the name stingray, instead of "gentle angel of the sea." What we humans do to animals?

Turtles:

If you swim with your arms fixed to your side, you can get close to most turtles under water. I have caught five turtles this way. They watch you and you watch them out of the corner of your eye making as if you are just swimming next to them, as you get within the right distance you shoot out both arms one aimed at the shell right next to his neck and the other right next to his tail, also on the shell, but your grip has to be firm, because the larger turtles spin round and round, trying to flip you off, like a crocodile spinning to break off flesh. I have spun around a good few times hanging on. Guests love to see this, then I let them go.

A Remarkable Ship Wreck Story:

As told to me by Barry Rice names have passed my small brain. The Bermuda triangle is Miami, Puerto Rico and up to Bermuda. Patrick and Joanne were in the Bermuda triangle on their way to Bermuda, when they were hit by a large storm, the waves were as big as hills and the troughs, as deep as valley gorges. The yacht rolled over with Captain Patrick on deck and Joanne down inside the yacht for protection. Once the first roll was done, Patrick was gone into oblivion and a washing machine of mountainous seas, totally impossible to survive in those conditions. Hours seemed like days and they passed, Joanne rose from her unconscious mind, she waded through 3 feet of sea water and debris inside the yacht's salon, with every bruised step of her battered body, she opened the hatch and looked outside. Blood trickled down he cheek from the cut in her hair. The deck was a mess of tangled ropes, wires, broken mast and ripped sails scattered around. No sign of Patrick. The salon roof had been ripped off the yacht when she rolled over. The salty taste of angry wind spraying in her face was still in full force. The waves had not died down completely so everything was still being shunted around even in this morning angry seas, but it was now a sane place to be when compared to last night. Patrick had gone overboard, now she was numb. She was tired of holding onto the wall and being knocked from the side of the bed in the cabin. The tv in the salon had bashed her leg during the night, is her leg broken, no she could stand on the leg? I am going to die, this thought kept running through her mind.

Later when it was light out-side she tried to see what she could do to sail the yacht, but nothing worked, so all she could do was drift along aimlessly hoping some boat would find her. The days came and went, so did the food and water. Nine days later a fishing vessel was illegally cruising in waters they should not be and spotted Joanne. The fishing vessel with Chinese crew picked up Joanne gave her a warm blanket and some food and hot coffee. They took her to the harbor in Bermuda and none of them could speak English, plus they were illegally there. As the fishing boat entered the harbor, she saw a man running along the dock towards the fishing boat. "Patrick, Patrick," Joanne had to be held back from jumping across to the dock and injuring herself, but her eyes were full of tears, the dock lines were firm in place and Patrick jumped onto the fishing boat into her sunburned weak arms. "You are alive, you are alive." Patrick explained that he spent the night sort of keeping alive by his inflated jacket and he had clung to part of the salon roof that was floating. He was in total darkness and never saw the yacht once he got to the surface, the huge waves were hitting him from every possible direction in the black of night. It was in the late morning when a small fishing boat picked him up and dropped him off in Bermuda. He had organized search and rescue to no avail, but he did hear that a fishing boat had picked up a stranded lady, so he simply had to wait to meet her on the dock, hoping the stranded lady was you. "I was making my way to the boat, which was about to dock when from a distance, I knew it was you, so I just ran as fast as I could to get to you."

August 2-8, 1995 from the Virgin Islands to Fort Lauderdale, USA:

August 8, 1995, at midnight, we docked and paid for the entire night at the fisherman's dock after a direct sail from the British Virgin Islands without stopping, to enjoy a silent night sleeping all of us. We were in the USA. The next day we cleared in and then docked at the Fort Lauderdale municipal dock for the first month. Two things were to happen at this dock that were most unusual. The first was a typical American car chase, where the one car obviously chasing the other overtook the other and served to a dead halt cutting off the other car and both cars were in the middle of our short road one stopped across, and in front of the other right in front of where we were docked. The driver's door opened and a magnum .45 was in one hand, as the driver ran over to the parked car shouting at a lady in the other car. We read in the newspaper that a man and his wife were fighting, when she ran in one car and he chased in his Trans-Am and: headed her off and drew a gun on her, and the police caught the man. Hello, America. We had formally arrived: in the Wild West.

Ladies Do Not Run in the Rain:

This paragraph may well save your life. All girls should read that statement again: Girls do not run in the rain but; rather get wet. The rain makes everything slippery. Duh. One night after a movie Gaile and I parked the car in the municipal car park and the heavens opened. Gaile made a dash for the catamaran and in the black of night I could not see her, but knew she was on board. We were at the municipal dock on the Inter coastal Water-way, which is black brackish water. This is a mix of sea water and the black fresh water from the mangroves. This is not an inviting place to swim. Where we are is the most uninteresting place to put your big toe into the water. Yuck. So Gaile disappeared into the night I locked my old Thunderbird and followed her onto the dock without seeing her. As I stepped across onto the deck of our catamaran Splendidum, I saw one of her shoes on the deck on its side and a second shoe on the trampoline. Red flag. The lights of our catamaran were not on, the second red flag. I walked along the sidewalk of the catamaran and went down two steps into the open cockpit to switch on the lights. No Gaile anywhere. Gaile where are you, Gaile, Gaile. Nothing just silence. "Gaile, where are you?" and now I am starting to panic, then I hear a very tiny voice. "I am splutter here. "I am here." I looked over the back of the aft deck and she was in this black water in the black of night next to the boarding ladder. The boarding ladder is on a swivel and never hangs in the water. It swiveled up and clamps to the deck so Gail was simply treading water and could not get out of the water, until the ladder was released into the water.

My wife, Gaile, has thin shoulder-length hair, so when she stepped out of the water, she looked like a drowned mouse. "What happened?" I asked, after I got a towel so she could towel off and go for a shower. "I slipped crossing from the dock to the catamaran and fell into the water." "No, you were running and jumped across in your haste and your foot flipped on the smooth finish of the wet deck and you fell six feet between twelve feet barnacle-filled wooden piers at 11.00 p.m. into the blackest dirty water. Yuck, do not run when it rains!" this is a good example of what can happen. Gaile could have drowned, and no one would find her body. There is normally a rip current in and out of the Intercoastal Water-way, but we were lucky there was no full moon and very little movement when Gaile fell into the black water that dark night. Girls do not run when the rain starts, but rather get wet. We could have lost an angel that night.

Ile of Venice: and Cobblestone Apartments, 1996-January 2000:

I think ever yacht arriving in Fort Lauderdale docks on the isle of Venice when they first start to settle into American way of life. Then we rented the yacht to two people and locked into a year's lease with an apartment named Cobblestone Apartments in Pompano and we were very close to a major highway the I-95 so was could see the north bound cars about eighty yards away from our second-floor apartment. Our verandah (porch) was the same level as the I-95 highway, which faced this busy highway, but that never effected our apartment way of life. I had been back to South Africa and needed a special stamp to be placed in my passport and could only do this by being present at the home embassy in person, so I flew home. Paul and Charlotte were friends of ours, I had met Paul at high school in 1958, so Paul suggested I stay with them for the week I was in Durban my home town. One evening Paul and Charlotte had a lady guest for Dinner named Silvia. Her husband had passed, and she was running a 7-Eleven type café in a bantu area. We were all around the same age of 58 years old. The dinner was good and the company even better. About nine months after this Paul called me to say that he Charlotte and Silvia, were doing a trip up to Jupiter and would be traveling along the I-95 and before they got near our Cobblestone apartment, he would call me as they passed so I could wave to them. This would happen in a few days, so it slipped my mind. One day I was working at the apartment and the telephone rang, "Andy," "Yes,"

"It's Paul, Silvia and Charlotte and I are going to pass your apartment complex in two minutes, can you stand on the porch and wave to us." "Sure." Paul had been to stay with us, so he knew exactly where this was on the highway. Facing the road to my left was a large tree and Paul knew to show both girls that just after the tree they would see Andy on the porch. On the floor above the ground floor, so the seconds ticked by. What could I do to make them remember this trip? An Idea shot through my mind, take off all my clothes and wave naked to them, so that is what I decide to do. With no clothes on, I stood on top of the porch table, so they would have a clear view of this naked man eighty yards away. There were forty seconds to wait and just then a Broward police patrol car went slowly along the access road within our apartment complex right below me. I stood dead still and did not move a fraction. Oh geez, imagine him seeing me there the TV news tonight would hear the words, "Naked man standing on porch flashing." Not to worry the patrol car went by and I nearly got down from my lofty perch, but I stood my ground. Then into view a slow car arrived and I heard two women bust out screaming at the top of their lungs "Whhaaaa!"" And their screaming carried on for at least a mile down the road. I had wiggled my body like a Hawaiian dancer, to highlight my waist area. Okay that was far more reaction than what I had expected, but it was so funny. Now, here is what Paul, driving the car, said what transpired from his side, and here comes a second very funny side to the same story. Paul pointed out the large tree before they were to see me, so both girls were looking out their windows expecting to wave to me. Just before the tree, Paul slowed down to a snail's pace and pulled to the side of the road. You will see Andy on the balcony waving to us, Bang, like the impact of an explosion, the interior of the car exploded into uncontrollable screams from both women. The loudest shocked screams any two woman can make, both heads leaning out their respective windows, reverberated within the vehicle. This shattering of the silence gave Paul such a fright. His judgement was impaired for a few seconds, he swerved and nearly hit the small boundary wall of the highway, then he over-corrected and ran into the slow traffic lane nearly impacting two other cars flashing past at fifty-miles-per-hour. Once he got sorted out the woman were still screaming at the top of their lungs. "Geez, what are you girls screaming at?" Paul had not seen Andrew. After hundreds and hundreds of yards the screaming simmered down. "Andy was buck naked and shaking his body, ha… ha." the screaming now turned into laughing. Every few miles Charlotte and Silvia would crack up again. Yes, that wave was worth hearing what happened inside their car. Both girls got an eye full of the most unexpected wave ever. Had they all not been such close friends, plus of all the same age, that would never have happened. That really was an eye opener for all.

Running from the law:

Cobblestone Apartments were built just after a large curve in the road and the police like to trap speeders right there. The police stand after the major entrance gate into Cobblestone Apartments, but there are two entrances one where the road completes that curve on a straight section and the driver can see all the way down the road to where they step into the road if the driver is caught speeding. The gate where I turn to go into our apartment block opens slowly and you can see all the way down to the major entrance. What I am about to say happened once. I came out of that long curve and as I straightened out a policeman stepped into the middle of the road 150 yards away from me, but my gate was ten yards from me, so I swung into my gate waited for it to open and knew the policeman was running as hard as can be. The gate opened and I went into our apartment block, well before the policeman got near to me. The apartment block is so large that it is silly to try to find one car inside. Okay, that is the one and only time in my life to have run from the police. No more Cobblestone Apartment, or Apartment stories.

A New Single-Family Home in Tamarac 2000 – 2019:

Tamarac is on Commercial Boulevard, which is one of Fort Lauderdale's major roads. Our boundary is west on Commercial Boulevard, so we are a suburb of Fort Lauderdale. I was now an established yacht charter broker and making waves within this industry. We had settled into our new home and ran our business out of the enclosed rear porch of our home. That was the very reason for purchasing the home. This house had a thirty-three feet by eighteen feet fully enclosed rear porch and that size was perfect for what I had in mind. I was going to various boat shows around the world to know my product, Monaco, Genoa, Greece, Antigua, New Port, and the Virgin Islands. This huge porch can serve as an office.

911 – September 11, 2001:

My best friend Jim Frey from the Caribbean who also chartered with us, with his first wife Connie, and then his second wife Tanys. Jim Frey was in the throws of getting married to Tanys Waldron. Jim is a big timid gentleman, who kindly asked me to be his best man, I said, "Yes." The date for their wedding was set to Saturday September 16, 2001. Gaile my wife flew into Kawlona, Canada two weeks earlier so Gaile was with the bride. Jim had paid for his flight to Kawlona for September 11, 2001, and I paid for mine, to arrive September 15, 2001 to arrive the day before the wedding. I was at work when my daughter Susan called and said turn on the TV. We did and the one twin tower in New York had been hit by a plane. At the early stage of this crash the TV commentator said a private plane had flown into the building. Our entire staff were watching the TV when a second plane hit the second tower and I said that is Bin Ladin and none of the staff had heard the name before. It turned out to be Usama Bin ladin. Big problem for Jim and Tanys. I called Jim and said I would not be coming as all flights had been closed. Here is Jim and Tanys's story. Jim and his dad were traveling to the airport at 8.00.a.m. to catch their flight later that morning and it was announced over the radio that the twin towers had been hit by two air planes. Jim turned around right there and went back home. Once at home he decided that he and his dad would start immediately and drive to Kawlona Canada 4,267 kilometers from doorstep to doorstep. The trip started immediately, dad and son drove through the night non-stop. Arriving at the Canadian border was an almighty issue, there was a line of cars trying to get to Canada 1 mile long and Jim knew he simply could not stop there as he would not make the wedding. So, timid, soft spoken, Jim all six foot two inches of him, walked to the front of the line and explained to the border guard that he was racing to get to his wedding. The guard said, "Bring your car to the front of the line," and big Jim went through. They were not sure if they would make their wedding at 2.00 p.m. on Saturday, but it was going to be close. Now from the bride's side of her dilemma, someone must have alerted the national Canadian TV and they aired the bride, explaining what had transpired, and here are the bride's words to Television news that day, two hours before their ceremony. We saw the entire presentation which aired that day so here are her words as best I can remember. "The groom, my man, is racing to be here from Alabama, and if he does not make the 2,00 p.m. ceremony I will marry him over our cellphone." There she stood in her full bridal dress determined as ever to get her man. Jim arrived one hour before the ceremony and got dressed in his all white navy outfit and they were married. Today they are visiting us in Fort Lauderdale and are just as happy as day one 19 years later.

Breaking into My Own Home:

I had just returned from some annual boats show and a friend was supposed to pick me up at the airport but after thirty minutes I picked up a taxi for $50 and got a ride home. The taxi driver dropped me at my door and was gone. The house was locked and closed so I had to break into my own home. I found a window, had to break the fly netting but could get in head first and on the inside was the bath-tub so, I slid down head first into the bath tub. Just then a lady appears in the doorway of the bathroom. "Andrew is this you?" "Yes Chloe," my wife's sister, Geez, that had slipped my mind, Gaile had said both her sisters would be at the house, I had forgotten, all I had to do was knock on the door. "Andrew Jennifer and I were so scared, we heard this person breaking in into your house, we did not know what to do, thank God it is you."

2001 Mell Jacobs Sailing Home:

I was running my charter brokerage company Barrington-Hall and I got a telephone call.

"Hi, Andy Mell here. I am in Fort Lauderdale, come and visit me." I went to meet Mell at his dock at 10.00 a.m. the next day. What a shock, the dock was full of parts of his yacht Classique, the motor, cushions, carpets, cutlery, and everything was in the sun, this looked like eight captains had thrown all their junk in one spot near Mell's yacht. I knocked on the hull and out came Mel, big smile. "Andy looking sheepish as normal," he said, "Last night I anchored in the cannel and while I was sleeping, the tide went out, the yacht went aground and heeled over making all the salt water ran into my boat through the side windows, (open port holes)." When I was inside the water line was five feet above the floor level on the one side and a few feet on the other. "Andy, I had to wait until the tide lifted us up so they could tow me to this dock." I have cleaned all the parts and they are just drying in the sun." Well that was Mell. As always Mell was by himself and he had done the thousand-mile trip by himself. "I am now going to get going and cross the Atlantic on my way to Europe and eventually back home to Auzzi-Auzzi. I have put an advert in the local newspaper asking for three girls to pay their way on a yacht across to Europe and they will be here soon. Andy you need to go." "No, Mell, I am going to stay a while longer to chat a little more." Then we heard a knock on the side of the yacht and Mel gave me that embarrassed smile again, I had seen this look in the past. There were three girls and each one had high-heels, mini-skirt, breasts shooting the stars, lots of make-up, and painted fingernails. "Geez, Mell, you just do not learn. These girls were so far away from sailing ladies, they too had zero idea what they were signing up for. I never saw Mell Jacobs again and I was very worried that he would make an ocean crossing in his trusty Classique. I did make calls over the years and did find out that Mell Jacobs had got home. Well done Mell, I hope yachting is totally out of your blood.

Susan's Cat Simba Chips:

Our daughter Susan had found a bump on her left shoulder the size of a ten-cent piece and asked me "Dad what is this?" I have no idea, "Suzie have the doctor look at it." The doctor told me she had the worst cancer known to man and she would be gone in six months. Susan changed her diet to green food, and she lived for two years. This was a very bad time for Gaile and I and worse for Susan. There was simply nothing as parents we could do, and doctors had given up and that lump had long past broken the skin to form a slimy wet smelly bump the size of a rugby ball that dropped and turned almost under her arm on the outside of her body we had to dress that smelly wet bump twice every day, then bandage her up. For the last six months of Susan's life, her poor cat Simba Chips was left much on his own. The cat was sort of fed in a bowl that never got cleaned and ended up as a night cat. The cat went out at night and came back to sleep every day. I loved the cat he was black and white, plus the cat was a Hemingway. All Hemingway's have six toes on each paw, and so did Simba Chips, but it was his character that appealed to me. We saw them come and take Susan's body away, and she was cremated. We also got to keep the jar with her ashes. Not good. I wanted Simba chips to be our cat, so I would go to Susan's house which was easily over one mile away across two road bridges, over water and through a mass of houses here in Tamarac, which is Fort Lauderdale in Florida. The first day I drove to look for Simba Chips, he was outside the Susan's home. 'Come on Simba, and he just stood there, I had to get out the car, walk over to him, pick him up, and place him in the passenger's side of the car." His head moving back and forth, smelling all the new smells and looking agitated. You could see what he was thinking. I had to jump in the car fast, as he had already walked onto the driver's seat, looking down at the open door. "Okay, kitty cat, up you come on my lap." I said, all in one swift move closing the door. Being a male, I knew he would jump out the window, so I cracked open the window just enough to have him place his head through the window, and with all four legs and his twenty-four toes on my lap, we headed for home.

When we got back home each day, Simba would eat his food, in a clean bowl, then slept the remainder of the first day. He ate his evening meal, flipped his tail in the air with a curve at the top of his tail and started to walk away. He was going home, to Susan's house, the only home he ever knew. How he knew his directions back to Susan's old house, I will never know. There are two bridges over water and it certainly is not a direct walk home as the crow flies. The next morning at 7.00 a.m. I went to Susan's old house, looking for Simba Chips. There he was stand next to the house, I called him and he started to walk away from me. I quickened my pace and picked him up. Simba was placed in the passenger's seat with a meow, head nodding. By the time I got into the car, Simba was on the driver's seat, so onto my lap he went, and the driver's door went closed. I cracked the window open, and we then drove home with the cat on my lap and his head out the window. When we arrived home, I opened my door and Simba was always first out the car, then straight to his food in his clean bowl. Again, he slept at his new home all day long and had his evening meal, and we saw that curved tail head back to Susan's old home. This went on for two years every morning. I never missed one day without going to pick up Simba Chips and it was my utter pleasure to do this. One day Simba Chips just did not brother to walk back to Susan's old house. I never had to go again. He got the message the love and caressing were right here, he did not have to walk a few miles every day to find love. When Gaile and I went away for a week-end, we would simply put out a bowl of food for him with some water. This was a cat who could look after himself in every way, so off we went. It was coming back home that has stuck in my mind forever. As we rounded the corner, we could see our house with Spanish tiles on the roof and a black cat patiently waiting for us on the roof. As Simba saw us, he ran over the roof to the back of the house, where we had a small shed. He could jump from the roof to the top of the shed and then jump to the green grass, his tail proudly in the air with that curve at the top of his tail, and he would be welcoming us at the driveway as we drove into the garage. Twelve years later I noticed Simba Chips was getting thin, and then clumps of hair started to fall off his sleek slim body. He was dying. I took my cat and put him down. I will miss Simba Chips curling up between my legs and falling asleep while I watched TV. That never happened during summer. It was too hot for that. I looked forward to winters.

The 2.45 a.m. Break-In:

At 2.45 a.m. Gaile and I were awoken by the sound of a huge smash followed by glass shattering in our lounge. Police have no clue what transpires when these things happen. They only see this from their side and what they see on TV. Here is what happened from our side. From the sound of what transpired, the huge crash and then glass shattering on our lounge floor. I felt I knew what was going on. People were in our lounge and somehow our large glass cabinet had fallen to the floor, making all our glass ornaments shatter on the lounge floor. I said to Gaile, "Come over to my side of the bed," and she did, so my body was in front of hers, plus I had pulled out my magnum .45, and I had the bed in front of me, and my outstretched arm with the revolver pointed at the door to our bedroom. When the burglars opened our bedroom door, they would be stone dead. I was in the dark and the robbers would be silhouetted. This is not a movie where you walk brazenly into the light giving robbers the advantage. I am in charge here. The movies and TV teach us how not to look for robbers in our homes. During any TV show the poor home owner switches on the lights and walks down the stairs, with light all-over themselves, making the hero, or the home owner the target and the bad dude tucked into the darkest shadow. The advantage is the robbers.

Gaile and I did the right thing. We went for a protected area in the darkest shadow and if anyone opened our bedroom door, then they would be dead. Gaile called 911 and while we were waiting, we could hear the wine of an A/C motor starting up then stop, then the wine would commence once again. It was something revving, not a vehicle, and stopping. After six minutes with gun trained on the door, I heard our front door bell ring. So I walked to the bedroom door, opened it carefully, and looked into the very softly lit lounge from the TV button. I then switched on the passage light, opening light into the lounge, and all looked well. No glass? Nothing was disturbed in the lounge? Strange. The doorbell went again, so I walked across the wooden floor of our lounge and noticed no glass on the floor and our glass cabinet was where it should be. I unlocked the front door to see a policeman and he said, "Are you holding a gun?" "I said Yes," "Give it to me." He emptied the chamber of bullets and handed both back to me. He said, "Someone has crashed into your house." I looked to my right outside to see a large SUV. Through our wall and through our front window, with the nose well into our home, the glass was piled up and the nose of this car behind our large curtain. When I walked through the lounge absolutely nothing could be seen to show me that anyone was in my home. Now I knew what had woken us up and how the glass was broken. The police were holding the man across the road one house down from me. Their story to me was he was also a policeman who had just finished two shifts and was going home to his mother (not his wife at 3.00 a.m.) after completing both shifts and had fallen asleep at the wheel. I knew this was baloney. It was a drunk cop who fell asleep and crashed into my home, and the police were protecting the man. Gaile and I should have been protected. Now I know what the revving was all about. This drunk man was trying to reverse out of my house, but he did not know he had a very big problem. His righthand front wheel was a small ball of crunched metal, with no tire on the wheel anymore. Within minutes a crowd had grown around my home and a tow truck had pulled his car across my grass to lift it up and tow it away. The police insurance tried to screw me with a refund, and I had not sued them, which I had not even though of. Had I known what I do now, I would have got going with a lawsuit. Gaile asked the policeman what we should have done in this case to protect ourselves. The police response was to switch on the light and see what happened. I told Gaile not to listen to his ignorance. "Just do what I did because I was right." We did everything correctly without being told. If you hear someone in your home, pull the gun out and stay in the darkest spot possible and wait for them to make a move.

To all TV lovers out there, a baseball bat is not protection.

SPORT: IS THE BACKBONE TO BUSINESS

Arab Story:

In 2014 for Christmas and New Year, both Gaile and I went home to Durban, South Africa to see family and as many dear friends as possible. Right at the beginning of our trip the aircraft landed in Johannesburg, so Gaile left for three days to spend with her sisters to enjoy the Kruger National Park, where they grew up, and I carried on to Durban. I knew there would be a crowd of pals (hooligans) waiting for me at the international exit, when I landed. I had not been home for thirteen years before that. Gavin and Belinda Sibbald, were a married couple from many years before, had set up a group of buddies to welcome me home. How could I foil them and walk right by them without them knowing I had passed all of them? My plan was to attack them from the back, while they were concentrating seeing me come out of the passenger's arrival gate. I thought to make two-foot-high stilts and to wear special long pants to alter my height, but the stilts would be confiscated before I boarded the aircraft. Okay, I purchased an Arab outfit, and this was perfect as I could also hide my face with only my eyes showing, and a pair of flip-flops would do well. I carried the Arab outfit in a plastic bag onto the aircraft and held it all the way to Durban. When we landed at Durban, I waited for everyone to get off the aircraft and then dressed in the Arab outfit. I walked up to the only two people in the aircraft the pilot and copilot handing over to the new shift and asked them if one of them could tie off the outfit at the back. I explained what I intended to do and they happily obliged. I asked them if I could walk with them out of the building as well and they said sure. I told them my plan was to get past my buddies waiting at the gate for me. They cracked up at what I was doing and said, "Sure walk off with us." So now off sets the "little Arab" with the pilot and copilot and we walked out the building together. I saw a huge sign, "Welcome home, Andy," so my buddies are there in full swing. I walked right past all of them and not one recognized me. I was not surprised. I could not take it anymore, so I stripped off my Arab headdress and shouted, "I caught all of you." They erupted with laughter. After many hugs I realized I had left my luggage on the baggage traveler. Now I had to get back into the airport.

So, I tried to go back into the baggage claim area, but the guard stopped me. "Sir, I just walked out of the gate but forgot my baggage?" Who would fall for that line? He did. I just walked in saw my one big suitcase standing all by itself and said, "This is mine," and walked out again. All was good, the guard let it all happen.

SECTION B

Now the business side of life follows:

February 1, 1962.

Okay, let's commence with my first day of work after I left high school: Below is how my up-bringing forged my life. Life for everyone has huge ups and downs. The easy way out is to succumb to drugs and drugs are normally started by Marijuana, so it is far better for you reading this book not to touch marijuana. If you already have experience Marijuana, make a pact with yourself never to touch that again. No drug should have any part of your life. Drinking excessively also has no part of your life.

Business and Climbing the Ladder:

My dad got me into a drawing office with the government; as a learner draftsman, and my interview went well. I got the job. I had to do night school, and my dad had always promised to buy me a small car when I started work, if I promised him never to ask for a motor-cycle, or to ride a motor-cycle. I kept that promise, and my dad got me a small Fiat 500, which seated four people, so now I could get to work and back. The drafting we did was mapping the telephone lines in the entire Durban area. My boss was Owen Stewart, who was an ex-lifesaver on the Scottburgh beach, but always a super ladies' man with soft blue eyes that simply drew in the girls. Owen was also a prankster and thirty-three years of age, and I was a naive small man of nineteen. I really enjoyed Owen.

I was to learn later in life Billy Barker had been killed in a road accident in 1961, but I had not heard of this until later years. Today I still cannot believe Billy Barker died so young. Owen, my boss was a charming, polite, fun, prankster, gentleman. He would walk next to me down the pavement, then grab my hand hard, so it was impossible to let go and gently swing both our hands, so we looked like two guys holding hands. I nearly died with embarrassment, but he kept holding on, with a straight face. Owen caught me again with another of his pranks later in the year, but he made everything sound so genuine. Here is great example of Owen playing tricks on various staff members. Tom Brown was going to do a verbal test to see how good his Afrikaans language was, and it was all set around written language and knowledge of his job, his plan was to pass to get onto a higher grade, with more pay at the post office. Tom had told Owen about the verbal test that was to happen the following morning. Owen told Tom that a favorite question was, "what is the name of a motor-cycle in Afrikaans? It is called a harkendak." Now remember harkendak. Repeat it to me harkendak. Owen went to the two people who would be testing Tom, the following day. "Hey John, I know that you are testing Tom tomorrow for his oral, but please pull a little joke on him when the test is over." "Okay Owen, provided it is in good taste and we can do it." "Yes, it is. When you have completed the test ask him what a motor-cycle is in Afrikaans, I have told him it is a harkendak." "Oh, geez Okay." The next day Tom nervously went in for his oral test of the language and the two men were sitting at the head of the table. Sit down Tom. Tom did his test and at the end the one gentleman asked Tom, what was a motorcycle in Afrikaans? Tom's eyes lit up and he shouted "A harkendak." Both men cracked up laughing and said, "No Tom go back and ask Owen what it really is." Tom Brown passed and got his promotion, but not without scolding Owen. I have used the exact name harkendak that was used that day in 1962.

I did hear Owen was very sick with cancer in 1987 (age fifty-eight years old) when Gaile and I went to see him, and we were very lucky we did, he passed two weeks after our visit. It was impossible to recognize Owen. He was thin, and all I could remember were his soft blue eyes. He said to me, "I am going to kick the bucket!" "Never," was my reply. "I know how to pop you out of the bed. Doctor Andrew has the only remedy." I called Gaile to stand at the end of the bed and said, "Now take off your top first, then the rest of your clothes." Owen broke down laughing, "I am not supposed to laugh, or cough, it is bad for me. Thank you for being my friend."

In the Army:

So, in 1962 I worked all year then went to the Army for a mandatory nine months, March 1 to December 31, 1963. It was clear to me I wanted to be the boss, so army life was not quiet my thing. All the soccer in the world was also enjoyed during army life. In 1964 I was back at work drafting. Also playing soccer for Addington who were the local hotshots, as surfing took over, I eased out of serious soccer into surfing in mid to late 1964.

Sonny Listen versus Cassius Clay, 1964 Miami:

In those days we listened to boxing fights on the radio, and we knew that Sonny Listen was going to beat the daylights out of the Louisville lip. Poor old Cassius Clay had finally met his match, the hardened ex-jail bird, in Listen. Jimmy Geddes, his brothers and sisters, Robbie Young, and I were in Umbilo Road crowded around the radio listening to the entire broadcast. Cassius Clay beat Sonny Listen. Wow, that was impossible, but he did to become world champion. I did not realize that one day I would live pretty close to where that fight took place in 1964.

Mobile Oil Refinery, 1965:

The surfing bug had bitten me hard. I started to look for a job that allowed me to surf more. In 1965 I went to work for the mobile oil refinery. There we had three mandatory shifts, 8.00 a.m. to 4.00 p.m., then 4.00 p.m. to 12.00 p.m. and 12.00 p.m. to 8.00 a.m. One full day between shifts and four days clear after three weeks. Lots of surfing time, also lots of shit work. There was another prankster in Joe Torin working at the refinery, and he played all kinds of jokes on us new guys during our first year, and I got many jokes played on me. We used to go for a smoke break at 4.00 a.m. into one of the open smoking areas and generally one puff and your eyes turned back from being tired, and you would fall asleep until the cigarette burned your two fingers, or until your head fell to one side. The head operator (Joe Torin) used a small car to ride around to various plants, and one night round 4.00 a.m. Joe spotted me sleeping, smoke in hand, so he free-wheeled his car, right up to within two feet of me, and switched on the lights and hooter, all at once. I woke up knowing I was being run over, by the car lights and horn blaring. Joe was breaking down laughing. I did get sick from the prank. I also thought that was funny. I was far too young to come up with something that would catch Joe. However, one night around 8.00 p.m. a friend of mine Johnny Kay and I were in two girls' apartment just getting to know them, but I told Johnny I needed to drop him off as I had to go to work, which I did. Before Johnny got out of my car, he said, "I took these panties from the girl's bathroom," "Geez, Johnny, what for?" He did not know why and left them on the seat of my white 1966 Ford Corsair. When I got to work, I drove into the staff protected car park and parked next to Joe's car. "His windows were open, so I flipped open his glove box and flopped the red panties into the glove-box and said nothing and walked to the control tower. I never thought of those panties again. That little prank I forgot for three months and one night at 2.00 p.m., all of us were standing around the main control counter. I remembered putting the panties into Joe's glove box. "Hey, Joe, did you ever find some ladies panties in your glove box?" His hand hit the desk with a hard smack on the solid table, catching everyone's attention, the soft hum of a happy refinery in the control room now dead silent.

"Andrew!" Joe is now angry, "Had I known it was you two weeks afterward, I would have killed you." "Joe, I am sorry, I will go and tell your wife what I did. I will honestly go and get that done right now." "Not necessary, it is all sorted out now. Andrew, let me tell you what happened, so that you will never do that again. As you know, I played the organ in a band and my wife was suspecting me of messing around with another girl. I told her she was being silly. That was a Sunday morning, so to clear the air, I suggested we do a drive in our car. Both of us got into the car, and we were ten, or twelve miles away from home when she opened the glove box and pulled out a pair of red ladies' panties. She turned to me holding these panties in my face and said. "Okay, who's are these?" almost screaming, "Yes you four-letter word, I got you." I looked at them. Totally dumb founded. "Who's are these, Joe Torin? Tell me Joe." "I really have no idea. And I have no idea how they got there."

"Stop the car."

"but honey," "Stop the car."

I stopped the car she stormed out and started to walk home with me in the car slowly riding next to her, then behind her. She would not get back into the car, "I will walk home Joe." So, she walked all the way home. "Andrew, never do that again you have no idea what drama you caused." "I will honestly tell your wife what happened, Joe." He said, "Not to worry, all was good." Joe and I always remained good friends even with me not thinking what could happen. Shift work ultimately irritated me, and I started to look for a eight to five normal workday.

1697-1970, Now to Penguin Pools:

I did get a few silly jobs along the way until Tommy Johns, Diane's husband, suggested I work at Penguin Pools as their draftsman, Alister Roberts, a dear friend from motor racing, was a school teacher and had been doing pool plans on the side, but they were selling far too many pools for Alister to keep up with, so they started to look for one full-time person to take over, and I got the job. Now I worked drawing pool plans Monday to Friday and overtime when needed, but no overtime pay. That was okay for me. The salary added up to $1 per pool and I was doing 110 pools each month and was on a fixed salary. Gaile and I had decided to get married February 28, 1970, so I went to ask the boss for a raise to $250 per month, minimum wage, he said he would think about it. I walked out on those words. Think about it. No sir, there is nothing to think about. I never went back. I went to every pool; company in our town of Durban and offered all of them to do their pool plans. At the rate of $15 per pool plan, and in my first month, on my own, I made $250 plus, I had wasted so much time going to all those pool companies, so I knew that having a clear hard-working month meant more cash money for me.

Up to 1970, Living in Durban North:

One Saturday afternoon, I had been asked to pick up a bride and take her to her wedding. I had a Ford Corsair, which was a gorgeous-looking white car. The Ford Corsair was manufactured in England and exported to South Africa for our consumption. I had to pick up the bride at her home, dressed in white, with white veil, and take her to the church on time. I was the right person for that. The night before round 8.00 p.m. I was going home in this built up area when my headlights caught a snake crossing the road. I stopped the car, leaving the lights on and went behind the snake with my headlights between the snake and me. This was a red-lipped herald and not venomous. I was not one to keep snakes, or to normally catch snakes, but I did know that both the red-lipped and white-lipped heralds were garden snakes and non-venomous, so I picked it up behind the head and jumped into the car holding the snake firmly behind the head. I started to drive with one hand and proceeded home. During the drive home, the snake made a desperate bid to remove its head from my grasp, and out came the head, and the snake dropped on the bench seat and then onto the passenger's side of the floor. The snake was gone. The following day I studied the car inside looking for the snake under the bench seat and in all the spaces a snake could crawl into. Nothing. I had to get dressed to travel to the bride's home, so off I went, hoping everything would be fine. How can you tell a bride on the weddings day in full dress there is a snake in the car with her, but it cannot be found? I picked up the bride at her home and a bridesmaid sat in the back seat with the bride, both looking the part. We got to the church on time, and the bride and bridesmaid exited the car with no regrets. Luckily for the bride, she was married and took her new husbands' car to their honeymoon, wherever that was. I never told them, but I did share that with my parents. I took the back seat out the car at home the next day and the snake had crawled all the way up to the very top of the inside next to the springs of the rear seat to be at the shoulder of the bride, but with sponge and leather between her and old snake. I let the snake go never to see the it again.

1970-1990, Apartment Blocks, Prestige Homes and Factories:

My business life started right here when I married my wonderful wife, Gaile in 1970, now in 2019 that was forty-nine years ago, and going strong. There is one thing in life men and women must get right the first go around, and that is to pick the right partner to wade through life. I certainly picked the best puppy out of the entire bunch. Here is one reason that made up my mind. I enjoyed her company and still do, and as a couple we got along fine. One Saturday night, I decided to do all-night fishing. There was a favorite fishing spot that Army personnel could fish from, at the base of North Pier in Durban. Gaile said she would like to come, and I said, "Okay, but know that there is no coming home at two or three in the morning, it is all-night fishing." She said, "Yes," she understood. So off we went. We packed our gear plus food and beverages for the night and went fishing. I cannot remember if I caught anything, but at 2.00 a.m. I noticed a chill in the early morning air and looked back at Gaile sitting well behind me shaking in the cold, not saying one word. Another hour passed colder and more shaking from Gaile. Not one of my girl-friends would ever do this. All would be in bed. Only my pal would come with me and stay the entire night, even shivering for hours and not one peep. To myself I said, "Andrew here is your lady to marry, sitting right next to you." I say to everyone getting married, make sure you get that decision done right, just like me, and rest of your life will be a dream.

The pool plans drawings grew to home additions and garage add-ons to full homes in time. But in the first two growing years Jim Cramer of the Durban Corporation assisted me by giving me sewer plans to follow up. The entire Durban area was to be set with the new sewer system and no more septic tanks. This meant that owner had to pay for an independent draftsman to draw up a sewer plans to link their homes to the Durban Corporation mains. Owen Stuart from the government drawing office showed me how to draw my first sewer plan. Now I got it. Each small area had to comply, and the late great Jim Cramer gave me a head started to flip over plans at $15 each. I soon had John Murphy join me and John remained with me from December 1970 to 1990 when I sold the company. John Murphy is a talented gentleman who drew house plans and factories plus large apartment blocks, so the business grew as more staff were added. When John joined me in December 1970, I had a decision to make. The decision was an easy one to make. Do I go out and see all clients and quote prices to clients, as well as gather all related information to draw the plan? Or do I sit in the office and draw all plans. This was a major decision, and it would have lasting effects on the amount of money that came into the business. Delegate. I knew to delegate plus it was vital that all my clients meet and see me. As the years passed, I ended up with three items to tell all my clients that other competitors never thought of. If the client wanted a bathroom added, I had a way to show them without making what we were doing more expensive. We would recess the bath-tub behind the outside wall under an arch-way, plus instead of the outside wall, we take a large window-pane one tile up from the bathtub, which means you can laze in the tub and look outside. To stop other people from looking in, when you are in the tub, we build a one brick thick wall, three feet from the bath-tub and take that onto the bedroom leaving enough space for a glass door off your master bedroom, so you can attend to the flowers in that small space. The glass makes your bathroom double in size. Then there is an addition to the entrance of the home that can be done making the entrance brilliant with a planter and a sky-light above the planter. Those two additions to any-one's home makes your house price almost double. Now with me representing my architectural drawing office, I could expand on staff. My major job was to keep all of them busy.

The year 1970 Gaile and I lived in an apartment in Point Road and I started saving to get out of there. By the middle of 1971 we bought the land in Loon Road and I looked for a builder to build the house for us. We moved in the middle of 1972.

In 1971 I also bought my first brand-new car a 1971 Hudson Hornet, a sleek orange car with big flared mudguards like the Javelin, but in those days, we never knew of the Mach 1 Mustang, or the Javelin's.

The business was called Drawing Service, and I moved into Payne's buildings on the fifth floor in West Street the main road in Durban a thriving city of four million people with high rises and fly overs just like America. Our little girls, Debbie and Suzie, were growing up and getting bigger. We lived at 50 Loon Road in Sherwood in Durban and the business paid for everything, plus we went racing again. Life always seemed to be asking for money at every turn.

At the end of 1979, when Suzuki offered me their new 1,100 Suzuki and no money was mentioned, I said, no thanks. Now I could concentrate on my large money home in Lower La Lucia. I had paid the land off in full for Lower La Lucia, and now we had a new home for 1980 in Umhlanga. In 1983 we sold our new home for $100,000 more than what we paid for it. So now we looked to build 20 Ridge Road Lower La Lucia. I soon learned it was more profitable building new homes, with the business being the cash flow to support what I was doing. We rented a home for a few months and moved into Ridge Road in December 1983 and sold in 1989 making $300,000 in that process and lived rent free, plus I had three other homes under construction.

1990 This is a gap I did no work as we were waiting for the catamaran to be completed and after that the Atlantic crossing and then another ten months enjoying, the Caribbean. We started chartering Splendidum in the British Virgin Islands. But sailing up to the British Virgin Islands our first island from South America was Grenada. This covered earlier in this book.

Grenada:

Grenada the windward islands, or the Spice islands of the Caribbean. This is the one side of the Spanish Main.

Cane Garden Bay

There are no waves in the British Virgin Islands unless a small north swell develops and breaks on Cane Garden Bay. I had two gentleman guests in my tender and the waves were breaking this fine sunny day. The three of us were coming back by hard bottom tender from catching one lobster and our catamaran was anchored in Cane Garden Bay. As we got close to the start of a wave build up, I steered the tender into the wave as if we were on a surfboard. The wave picked us up and we were also surfing. This was great and I was to learn that both men had never done this before. The face of the wave picked up big time and hit the reef below. when that happens, the wave breaks sooner than anticipated and it was going to break before I expected it to. Luckily for me we were near the shoulder of the wave, and it curled so close to us it lifted the back of our tender up the face of the wave, but we shot out the wave right there. "Wow," was the sigh of both men, they thought they were going to be flipped over. "Guys, you are in good hands." My thoughts were, "Big Deal Andrew that was too close."

I would take my clients to places other Captains never went to. There were four sixteenth century cannons in ten feet of water on the safe side of the Coulequan Barrier Reef, and all my guests would get to take a picture or two of themselves touching the cannons. The cannons were placed there by Burt Kilbride, a gentleman I got to know and a close friend of Jacque Cousteau. The scuba dive shop near the Bitter End yacht club is called Kilbride's. Burt was an avid scuba diver and treasure hunter. He found the wreck of the *Sant Ignacus* which was a guard ship and he took these smaller cannons and placed them on the inside of the Coulequan Barrier Reef, so day snorkelers could see cannons under-water. These same cannons were there in 1990 and up to 2007, but I have not snorkeled there since.

SPORT: IS THE BACKBONE TO BUSINESS

I was invited to Burt's home in Tampa around 2005 and he told me he got gold from that ship-wreck. I am not sure if he was boasting, or not. Burt must have passed by now. My favorite spot to take snorkeling guests is on the outside of the Coulequan Barrier Reef, two hundred yards east of the Bitter End Yacht Club. Taking guests to the outside of a barrier reef can be dangerous, but not here because the Virgin Islands has only fourteen inches between spring high and spring low tides. This means no under tows (or currents) guests must worry about. Even on a windy day with small sea-horse caps, it is gorgeously still in forty feet of crystal-clear water. I would take simple snorkeling guests out there, dive down secure the anchor of the tender and have everyone jump into the water and follow me. Now you can see why a barrier reef is called a barrier. That living growing coral has grown up forty feet like a straight wall, facing that open ocean, so that each coral polyp can get every bit if food possible. This is where those rainbow-colored fish hang out, and this is where those large lobsters play. One day I looked left and saw a turtle swimming eighty feet from us, I turned right and eighty feet in the opposite direct, a stingray glided out to sea. Guest and I can see eighty feet in all directions, so guests can clearly see no danger from sharks or any other underwater item. "There is no danger, no currents, so just enjoy what you are seeing below the surface and follow me." I point out a forest of stag horn coral, brain coral, soft-colored corals, and porcupine fish. On three occasions during these snorkeling trips I caught three turtles with my hands, and one was four feet in diameter. We took picture and let them go. There was one occasion that my guests were with me, and we were enjoying the most gorgeous day snorkeling this deep spot, I was ahead of them a little and had seen the largest shark, I had ever seen. This was not a tame nurse shark, it was a real big one, with dirty big teeth-protruding from its mouth. It was in shallow water ahead of me and flipped over the top of a little ridge, and I followed. I could see twenty-five feet over the next ridge and the shark had covered that distance to disappear. I could not see him at all, so I swam back to my guests in deep water and asked if they were ready to go back to Splendidum and their surprised answer was yes. All of us went back to the tender and jumped into the tender. I started the motor and said, "I did not want to say anything while we were in the water, but I saw my first real big shark in very shallow water."

"Andrew thank you for telling us when we were in the water. We would have panicked. We are delighted to be out, the water, but it was so gorgeous down there."

In all my deep-water snorkeling in the Virgin Islands I have never seen a shark that worried me. There are plenty of nurse sharks with no teeth, and there has never been a shark victim (or someone bitten) ever in the Virgin Islands.

There is a theory of the bath-tub effect. The Virgins is on a geological fault and all islands, except one, are volcanic. The maximum depth is one hundred and fifty feet, and this is not deep in any form. One mile from Peter island is a seven-thousand-foot drop-off, and it is felt that sharks are found in the deep water not in the top shallow water. So, they say, but for five years I snorkeled all by myself in sixty feet of water and most were open ocean, to my back. Most times there was no one else to go with, so it was either go and have fun, or get sun-tanned.

We left chartering on August 2, 1995.

Selection of Your Business Name:

Arrived in Fort Lauderdale August 8, 1995 at midnight, then opened Barrington-Hall in December 1995. One of the major problems I had with coming to America was being allowed to stay in the USA and to work in the USA. I had passed standard eight in South Africa, and that is equivalent to standard ten here in the USA. The emigration lawyer I hired to get Gaile and me into America told me I had to have a university degree. However, my twenty years of running my own architectural business, plus the fact the South African Architects association had given me exemption 13 certificate, which meant we were certified to design any structure in South Africa. I had employed staff that had been with me for twenty years and fifteen years, so the emigration lawyer asked me to get letters from various engineers who had worked with my company dating back a good few years. This was done. The emigration lawyer took everything to the dean of the University in Florida, who confirmed that anyone running a business for twenty years with staff; was just as qualified as any degreed person, so Gaile and I were on the right path to get our green card. We were lucky we could work here in the USA and at the same time do everything needed to become American citizens. This all took fifteen years.

I had a decision to make when I got here. Do I apply to work as a draftsman, or do I become a yacht broker? This new field appealed to me more than drawing plans again. Now I had to think of a name for my company Andrew Buys Yachts did not have the right ring to the name, so I selected Barrington-Hall Yachting Professionals Worldwide. It sounds like a big reputable company and that is exactly what I wanted to portray. Now I had my name.

We have serviced many film stars and celebrities over the years, thanks to the name of my company, but the biggest payback from the name is from a striving airline company. This company sell fix wing planes, jets, helicopters and have a maintenance division, one of the presidents is a YPO (young professionals' organization). You can only be a YPO if, before you are thirty years of age, you have started a business and turned over one million dollars. The other directors sell a lot of these aircraft annually. They felt that the same people I deal with, are also the same people they sell aircraft to. Apparently for years their happy clients have asked them; why they do not sell them a yacht as well? So, they started to look for a company they could be associated with. Barrington-Hall had sold a one-week charter to one of the CEOs. The material I had sent him had so impressed him, he felt that Barrington-Hall would be a great fit for his company. I got a call and a meeting was set up with five heads of their company and me. Barrington-Hall has always retained a License to sell yachts and kept this valid for many years, and I had used it five times when selling charter yachts. Their airline company need my license, so rough plans were put in motion and contracts signed. Today three of their CEOs work independently with Barrington-Hall as salesmen, to earn their individual salesman's license, then they can go their own way, or they can remain linked to Barrington-Hall. This bridge will be crossed when their contract is up. Here it comes, eight months later we are working on one yacht to be sold for forty-two-million-dollars, the commission we must split with another company. This is how important your company name is to you. The name *Barrington-Hall Yachting Professionals* was what attracted this company to my company. There was a very good chance that this would go through, because this yacht belonged to someone all of us know, and he wanted it sold to purchase a larger yacht. The prestige importance of owning this yacht had an attraction that wealthy people like to enjoy, as well. Currently, as of this writing we are hard at work with a purchaser. I do feel this will go through. The selection of my up-beat company name is the single most valuable part to get another company to be associated with us. They could have selected any other company out there.

1995 to 2018, Becoming a Yacht Charter Broker:

The very first boat show I went to, I was so proud to be a new broker, as I knew all the brokers out there and all of them were very nice to me, when I was a captain doing charters. Now that I became a broker they all felt I was a threat to them, this I found out later. I had set up a resort and Voyage catamarans plan with these two different companies. The resort, the Renaissance Grand Beach paid for an advert in a magazine that cost $3,200 each two months, for one year. The magazine had given me a copy in color on a hard board, to me to keep in my office and I brought that along to the annual Antigua boat show. I placed this nice large color advertising board in the salon of this Voyage catamaran, that I was sleeping in. This was at the 1997 Antigua boat show. The first morning I awoke with the sparrows, as normal and went for a short walk, looking at the various yachts along the dock. I saw a gentleman I recognized but had no idea who he was, so I walked up to him walking his little dog. "Hi, Good morning." he did not look up so I raised my voice and got closer, because I was eager to say hello and I knew he would hear. "Hello sir, good morning," I said again, and I knew he clearly heard me. His head down, making out as if he did not hear me. Oh well he had a problem, so I went on my way, and headed back to my catamaran to dress for the day and walked ashore for breakfast. That night I noticed the same man and his wife were also on board the same catamaran as I was. Now I remembered the gentleman his name was John, and his wife was a broker named Pat. "John, this morning I walked up to you and said good morning, you did not answer me."

He mumbled sheepishly, "Yes I did hear you." But with head down and not proud of having to answer that question. OH well, I originally thought he was a nice man and I liked Pat. We finished dinner around 9.00 p.m. on the catamaran, and we were sitting around all with drinks in hand when Pat blurted out the following words, and louder than normal, so her words catch every ones ears the captain and his wife are present. "Do you know what I hate about this industry?" said Pat. "What?" "I hate it when a captain becomes a broker and takes all my business." That statement was directed at me. I took my right hand and hit that fiberglass table with force, "Pat you booked me once in five years. You are a charming, soft-spoken, easy-going lady, and many people enjoy doing business with a person like yourself. They like your easy-going manner, your certainly are not pushy. I am on the aggressive side and like to lead people into my way of thinking, which other people enjoy. You as a broker, should be thanking me for opening a fresh avenue to grow the broker business, and I left the table and went to bed."

I was in bed when I heard a knock-knock on my door, and it was the captain. "Well said Andrew, you certain put that across in a nice way." Her pettiness had show her stripes.

In 1997 I was going to join CYBA The Caribbean Yacht Brokers Association, but one clause they had in joining was; that all brokers had to place all clients' money in the CYBA' brokers American account in the States. That would not do for me. One broker running that bank account could run away with millions, and we would all be paralyzed. I elected not join CYBA. That to many brokers was a kick in the face; by me, but I knew my clients' money would be far safer in my escrow account, than in theirs. All twenty-three years of me doing business, I have not belonged to the CYBA association. This did not sit well with many of them. My clients have always been protected. From time to time I have heard that their state side bank has paid late, and missed payments along the way, but overall, they have done Okay. Okay is not good enough for Barrington-Hall, we are never late with payments.

The next story is one of spite, and how to change spite into my favor. One broker lady did this to me on three different occasions and each time I got the contract. What I am about to share with you is how to change spite into my advantage. I was dealing with a charming lady client, explained all the details, that needed to be done and enjoyed during and before doing her charter, plus I had given her four yachts to select from, then no contact for six days, by my client. The telephone rang six days later, and here is what she said to me. "Andrew, I have no desire to do my charter any-more, said my client to me. "Why?" "I have just been speaking to another broker, Mrs. Blah, and she tells me, no one likes you, and you are this, and that." I answered, "That Lady Broker, is normally a very charming lady who I liked, and something must have happened to her today that you and I have no idea what is, so she is not thinking normally and both of us should not judge her actions now."

"Gee, Andrew, you are right, send me the agreement let's get this charter done."

I never run-down fellow brokers, rather build them up.

The same lady broker did that three times. She also lost three deals being nasty.

One gentleman asked me to go home to South Africa and he was one of my favorite brokers. In my first few years I was already booking more charters than most of them. Yacht Charter Brokers are very insecure with their position, because ten brokers book 70 percent of all the charter business which enters our industry, and the insecure group do not fit into that top ten brokers. For twelve years I was North America's third largest booking broker. It did not take long to knock the largest booking lady broker off her stool, and that started an eruption. She lasted four years after me booking more charters than her, and she retired, not without starting a good few untrue rumors. During my various visits to boat shows around the world and boarding the world's largest and most exotic yachts, which were asking to be chartered. I would take my own pictures of all cabins, saloons, kitchens, the outside sunning areas, and the crew. At most annual boat shows I would see a minimum of fifty different vessels. Once I got back home, I would sit down with my internet guru and make one small picture web site for each boat. For at least the first eight years I was the one and the only broker taking my own pictures of the yachts and was always puzzled why none of the established brokers did this as well. Once you have boarded three yachts in a morning it is impossible to remember what the first one looked like unless you have pictures of them. Even today I feel naked without a camera, since the invention of the cell phone. I notice brokers taking pictures and even now this is few and far between. People are lazy, so the sports-man, or sports-lady, can take advantage of this laziness. Some yachts are so-over-the-top with gold everywhere, gold taps, gold railings, just far too much gold on-board. I have been on-board one yacht with a sixteenth century Stradivarius in a glass case, an original Van Gogh painting. I would say the most historic yacht remains the Christina 0. This yacht belonged to Aristotle Onassis; Jackie Kennedy, Jack Kennedy, Blue Eyes, Sir Winston Churchill, Maria Callas and Marilyn Monroe, were some of the guests on board. Today the yacht has been refurbished and is magnificent inside, the swimming pool was also used to keep Aristotle's lobsters and doubled as a dance floor. The bar stool's leather seating was manufactured from whale foreskin. I enjoyed beers at this bar and a dinner in the most gorgeous dining room on-board the Christina O. The most magnificent dining room I have ever enjoyed a meal was Mussolini's favorite dining area in Genoa. We were invited to this huge nine-hundred-year-old hall in the center of Genoa. There are Michael Angelo paintings on the ceiling and thin bird netting to catch any plaster that falls from the ceiling. You can hardly see the thin netting. The ceiling is seventy-five feet from the floor, the walls have statues, and there were Roman columns all the way around the hall and the front of this huge hall, is a stage so those tables were higher than we were. All the serving staff were old men dressed in white-gloved uniforms. We were served a four-course meal. Gaile, my wife, was with me, and she hardly ever attended annual boat shows. So, after these high-end annual boat shows, I would end up with millions of pictures, when one day my internet gentleman suggested, "We not only make these many small web sites for you Andrew, but we also give all your information to every broker in the industry. The one draw-back Andrew, is we would be putting all brokers on the same level as you?" That never phased me in anyway, "Nah, that's OK."

"The good news is, we make them pay you for all this information." This is how Central Yacht Agent was born. Yes, all central agents, boat owners and advertisers were paying me monthly fee for this service. I did sell this company off to an interested party and I still use Central Yacht Agent database daily. Here is what Central Yacht Agents did and still does for me today. I pay as a normal subscriber each year to use their service. A client calls us asking for a yacht to charter. We take all their contact information and where and what they wish to do during their week on board. Now we look up all the yachts within the client's same budget, and automatically twenty yachts pop up for me to select from. I then select four or five and send that to my clients. I can be sleeping, and the Greek yachts automatically update rates, crew, pictures through their own agents, on my company web site. This never happened in our industry before 2001, so this has been a great tool to enjoy for the past seventeen years. I did sell this company in 2017. Central Yacht Agent database is the only worldwide American charter database in the world. There are two other databases, one English and the other French. Central Yacht Agent boosted this industry from inception. Before we had Central Yacht Agent database our company could only do three packages each in one day. We had to call the yachts central agent and ask them if the yacht was available, they would ask for an e-mail to be sent to them, with all the details. Only then would they call and ask the owner if he wanted to do said charter. The boats central agent may not get the owner for two, three, four, five days, or never, so we had to make multiple calls, just to ask that question. The system was so antiquated. Today we can do fourteen packages each day, as everything is automatic. There are still problems because some agents have no idea how important all the details are, that need to be placed on Central Yacht Agent database. Clients cannot wait all the time those central agents were expecting paying customers to wait for answers. We can do fourteen almost every day. We no longer must call and ask each company for all these details, the vital details we are looking for is right in front of us twenty-four hours a day, seven days a week. In the first two years most pictures were mine, plus we also had pictures and crew profiles, plus the specific chef's menu, as an example. Not easy to get everyone on-board, even the largest most well-established companies out there, did not get it. They will eventually get on-board. I did sell that section of my company, so I no longer own CYA. I am trying to slow down, but find that difficult to do, as I have been so active.

Trying to Be Nice.

One evening at an annual Greece boat show there were always ten women to one man. To me this is a good thing. Any way we were on-board a yacht, Sir Winston Churchill, laughing enjoying a drink, or two, with happy-hour treats. I saw a gentleman standing all by himself, as if he was excommunicated from this show. So, I walked up to him to ask him if he wanted to join me and the ladies at the happy hour table. I wanted him to share in the good people I knew. As I got to him, he turned and said to me, "Gee look at that sunset, it is magnificent." "Yes, it is, Sir!" I asked him to join all of us at the table and he told me his name and I told him mine. I did not anticipate his reaction; "My wife is Blah- blah and we certainly want nothing to do with you." Oh well, I do know his wife, and in my entire career, I had done absolutely nothing to harm her, but she never booked many charters in her life, so her nose must have been out of joint from that. I was to learn later her husband passed away a few years later and I have not seen her around for a good nine years.

I have enjoyed all the boat shows and most of my fellow brokers. This is a difficult business and few people survive a couple of years, you cannot treat this business as a part-time job. This is a full-time position and needs 100 percent of your attention, always. The major idea of this book is to show everyone that a sportsman, or sport-lady have the right backbone and habits to run any businesses. Sports is team work. You better be punctual and take pride in your work ethic. Your politeness is something you need in Business. Luck offers itself, only when you make things happen, like working hard each day. Many so-called brokers are just order-takers, they work for a large company with unlimited advertising budget, but the independent charter broker must go into the world of business and solicit one-week yacht vacations to the entire public at his or her own cost.

In my years as a yacht charter broker, I have visited annual boat shows in Monaco, Genoa, Greece (fifteen times) Antigua, St Martin, Tortola plus the United States Virgin Islands, Newport, Miami and Fort Lauderdale boat show. I have paid for the 2019 annual Barcelona boat show where the world's top charter power yachts will be. At every turn in my life, be it when I felt low; or on a wonderful high, my wonderful wife, Gaile, was right next to me. She never judged. She just built me up and a strong character like mine needed an equally strong, loving lady by my side. I am so grateful to have selected the best wife any man could ever hope for. It is clear I was her MMWC and she was my MWWC (Main woman what counts).

Spearheading Private Yacht Charters in China:

In 2005 I was invited to China by Martel Brandy, Mercedes Benz, and one other company. At the time they were also telling me what a big vibrant wealthy sector the Chinese had, and they were right for the charter industry. Their plan was to educate the Chinese people into the art of the private yacht vacation. This is where one family bonds their one-week, or two-week vacation period; of selecting one of the world's top hideaway locations to enjoy. I was driven to and flown to Shanghai, Shenzhen, and Beijing (at their expense) to have talks as well as show a giant-screen videos, which I had brought from Fort Lauderdale. Television, and radio covered each talk and stop. There were other companies who also gave talks, but not one had any kind of ten by ten-foot video screen, or videos and no competition. The videos I brought were of a captain introducing guest to

SPORT: IS THE BACKBONE TO BUSINESS

four top crew and then walking guests through his 130-foot yacht, first going through the salon, then the dining room and then all the cabins. I had three different videos, and all were short and sweet three-minute videos. We stayed at the top hotels in China and today I rate the Chinese cuisine as the world's best cuisine. The one resort/Marina/Hotel surpassed everything I have ever stayed in in my life. It was in Shenzhen and was brand-spanking-new at the time I did hear it had closed afterwards.

One would think that this was a successful trip. When I got back to my office, I had a good few calls and every call was from a person who was not used to the American way. Our industry is guided by the following definition. "Any vessel between fifty and five-hundred feet that sleeps a maximum of twelve guests. The Chinese were asking for thirty or forty guests to sleep on board, well that is cruise ship business. They would listen to the price and always offered one third the weekly rate, plus no APA (advanced provisioning amount.) The Chinese do not realize that owners do not budge on rates. The owners give all yacht brokers a base rate of $80,000 plus an APA of 35 percent. The APA is estimated to cover all expenses during a typical one-week charter, so that weekly rate would be a total of $ 108,000. The base rate would be $80,000 + $28,000 = Total $108,000. The independent owners of these private yachts are multi-millionaires who are not about to give reduced rates. This one point is the biggest obstacle the Chinese have. They will not pay the sticker price. After all that effort not one charter materialized.

The moral of my small note here is. The Chinese are nowhere near ready for the American's private yacht vacation. The effort to educate them will take many years and lots of money to do. Without this education, I feel the Chinese charter market is thirty years behind the Americans.

The Chinese yachts I saw were thirty and forty feet and very few. To me there is no Chinese charter market for the Chinese population as of today. The Brazilians and Russians are light-years in front of the Chinese when it comes to charter vacations. The Chinese have a vibrant small craft manufacturing market, which rest on their low labor rate, but generally those larger private power yachts are manufactured in the USA. The USA is the largest private power yacht manufacturing country in the world. There are a few European builders of power yachts over the size of 115 and larger.

Viking Story:

In May 2018 I was off to Greece and decided to stop for four days in Palma Mallorca, where my daughter and son-in-law live with our two grand-children, both boys seven and eight years old. Richard and Debbie are the parents to Alexander and Spencer. I asked Debbie not to tell the grand-children I was coming she said she could not do that, so I said, "Okay tell them I am coming three weeks later." and she said, "Okay. So, the kids are not anticipating my arrival. What could I do to surprise them? I went into a party shop and found an outfit of Vikings. But this Viking outfit was very special. The hat was glaring itself, by the two large horns on top of the helmet, but there was also a large bear skin coat with six-inch fur that draped over both your shoulders and completely covered the entire chest area of your body. Now that was good, plus I purchased two shiny chrome four-foot plastic swords. Okay, two sets of Viking outfits were purchased and now I am set for the grand-children, Alexander and Spencer.

The day arrived and we traveled first to the one school at 2.00 p.m. to pick up Alexander, but I planned with my daughter to have my back to the boys and stand around the corner twenty feet away from the mothers. I plan to have my back face the first kids as each got out of school, so that this strange figure attracts them. Once that was done and the kids are attracted, I would walk around the corner still with my hairy back to them and tap the high wall in front of me growling like a mad man. Okay, the plan was set, and we were in full hairy costume; The wives told me the first boys were about to come out of school. As the boys reached their parents, one boy spotted me, he leaves his mom, and shouted. "There is a Viking." I heard this pitter-patter of little feet running to get closer to me. I turn and disappear around that corner and as I did that, my back still facing the kids, – the first kid must have got a little fright, because he ran full speed back to his mom screaming.

"That is a real Viking, and then to his buddies, there is a real Viking around the corner, and he is big." Now three boys followed his lead and Alexander was one of them, all running closer to me. I am growling and tapping the wall with my gleaming sword. The one boy pulled at my clothes and I turned around and Alexander screamed, "That's my grand pa!" and he jumps into my arms for a big Viking hug. Alexander wore that Viking outfit from that moment on for the next three days to school and at home. Both boys got their Viking outfits.

Seeing Movies Being filmed:

I remember the movie "The Substitute" being made on the beach-front in Fort Lauderdale. The scene was the lady school-teachers' leg was being broken by the school bully in her class. I was in my first car an old Thunderbird and drove past in one lane slowly looking at the scene and later to saw the movie. Since living here, I have seen a few movie scenes.

Also, a week-end at Bernie's, but we were in the Virgin Islands at that time.

Baloons:

Gaile and I met a South African lady named Lynn on e-mail. Lynn, lived in Canada and was also from South Africa. We suggested she pop down and stay in our beach side apartment for a week which was open at the time. This way Lynn could have a week free and swim, either in the pool which was on the beach, or open the gate onto the beach and swim in the sea. Gaile and I would take her out every second evening and during the other days Gaile would take her to famous landmarks and also just walk the beach. Lynn said, yes she would love that. "When I arrive at the airport how will I know who you are" "Not to worry, Lynn, we will be holding a balloon" Gaile and I popped down to the airport with our large red balloon stretching up into the air. We walked around the corner to the arrivals waiting area, and there were hundreds of people and everyone had balloons.

I have never seen so many balloons in one place. These billions of balloons were certainly going to confuse Lynn, how was Lynn going to pick us out? Going to the gents toilet meant all the guys were holding balloons, now that's a first. I went up to one lady and asked why they had balloons and she said, "Everyone is waiting for their children who had been to a summer camp for 25 days." So everyone was waiting for their children. Some had multiple balloons and there were a few escaped balloons that had floated to the ceiling above. I did not see that coming. Gaile and I laughed about the incident, but we kept on waiting for Lynn and finally she walked straight up to us and said, "I just knew it was you when I saw you two standing here" So all was good we met Lynn.

Summary:

I have not worked for a boss since 1970 and have run two businesses and our life has been magnificent, full of love, fun, family and a good few warm friends. We have also had our ups and downs, but I believe our lives have been ten times more rewarding than working for a boss. I honestly believe that the sports side of my life groomed me for business, it provided the firm backbone needed for the business-world.

A teacher at high school: The summary of life.

This lady teacher picked Johnny Kay (the good Johnny Kay, as there were two. One Johnny Kay was a real bad dude, the other my pal). Any way the teacher asked him to stand and answer a few questions, "Mr. Kay, tell me what you would do if you found yourself in a thick, dense, high jungle?"

"I would walk around trying to find my way out."

"Okay, now you came upon a stream in the thick jungle, tell me what you find?"

"The stream is a dirty brown and I cannot drink the water. I can cross it and carried on walking."

"OK sit down."

SPORT: IS THE BACKBONE TO BUSINESS

Andrew Buys stand up. "You find yourself in a thick jungle, what do you do?"

I look for a huge dead tree and climb way up there and look across the jungle to see what direction I need to go in, to get out."

"OK now you stumble on a stream in this jungle, tell me what you see?" "The stream is crystal clear, and I can drink the fresh water, then I keep my direction and eventually find my way out the jungle."

Teacher to the entire class: "Class, the jungle is the big business-world out there. You have heard two different ways how they are going to work their way up the ladder of business. Wandering around is not going to cut it, Mr. Kay!" Andrew, that dead tree is perfect. It tells me you are going to have a weak, or bad start to your business field, it is going to be tough, but your way out is clear, and you will raise upwards.

Now that stream in the jungle Johnny Kay, you have a dirty mind, Andrew the clear water stream is the sex and relationship you have in life, and that is all encouragement to strive ahead in the world, after your weak, but right start."

The teacher was 100 percent correct with both Johnny Kay and me. I flopped around until I found my wife, I feel my life did take a similar path upward, but only after selecting the right partner for my life, and that was my wife, Gaile. Everything started once I got married to the right lady. I had the courage to start on my own, which also lead to racing motor cycles again and to other sports in my life. To me there is a definite relationship with sports and the business world.

I commenced this book with the red rose petal, because it was about spreading Susan's ashes and I ended this book with the same type of co-incidence about Susan. My wife, Gaile, had found a lovely picnic spot for Gaile and all our family to celebrate her fiftieth birthday to be held May 3, 2000. At Gaile's fiftieth Birthday party was Susan, Debbie, Dale, Mel, Loren (my sisters' daughter) and one other couple from South Africa, who were passing through, plus Gaile's best friend Beverley. I took the picture. This park is a gorgeous park with one-hundred-year-old trees for shade and lots of palm trees, and the entire park is well grassed. Everyone is in this color picture plus one park bench in the top right- hand corner. It was an accident this bench was in the picture, but it is there. The name of this gorgeous park is the "Colee Hammock Park" right in the middle of Fort Lauderdale. Susan had passed away in December 17, 2004, then in 2005 Debbie and Gaile approached the parks board and asked if a plaque be placed in memory of our daughter. The parks board said yes and Gaile and Debbie paid for their park bench. There are nine or ten parks around Fort Lauderdale, and the park the Parks board selected was the "Colee Hammock Park," and the bench they selected was the one bench in the top right-hand corner of our picture and that same picture had Susan in the picture as well as the same park bench. This little fact was only found in 2018 when Gaile and I were going through our family album in June 2018. That picture was taken four and a half years before Susan's passing. The plaque reads, "Susan Buys Jordaan 1973-2004 *Flying with Angels.*"

A guardian angel has always looked after me and my family over all these years, and for that I am eternal grateful. The one bad spot was losing our thirty-one-year-old daughter to cancer.

Opportunity never just comes knocking at your door. You must break that door down by hard work, only then does opportunity and luck grace you. **To view extra pictures related to this book enter www.arcbsports.com to your internet browser, then click to open.**

THE END

CPSIA information can be obtained
at www.ICGtesting.com
Printed in the USA
JSHW020853101119
2340JS00003B/6